PRAISE FOR
THE POISON GIRL

"Is *The Poison Girl* myth, legend, an immigrant daughter's tale, a Borges-like labyrinth, a culinary report on herbs and plants, or the edgy world of a young woman's escape from her father? It may be all of these at once. The novel is a wonder.... Written in brilliantly lucid chapters, it captures the imagination and, deservedly, the reader's admiration."
—Gary Soto, author of *The Elements of San Joaquin*

"Suzanne Manizza Roszak's haunting prose and shifting perspectives expose the psyche of damage. There are the lurking poisons of neglect and loss and violence. There are the temporary antidotes of fragile friendships and fleeting connections. And throughout, a family's history courses. The staccato moments that make up *The Poison Girl* resonate as a healing whole—quietly hopeful, deeply human."
—Adam Berlin, author of *Belmondo Style*

"A stunning work richly imagined, and veined with sentences so bright and alluring Manizza Roszak might have crafted them from a rare poison. This is an original and dynamic novel, a potent meditation on the mysterious and far-reaching bonds of family, a true work of art."
—Peter Kispert, author of *I Know You Know Who I Am*

"In a story older than its telling, Manizza Roszak tells the tale of generations of women poisoned by a world that wants them to be a possession or a weapon, but who wish themselves instead a medicine, a balm, a spell toward new beginnings. Visceral and haunting, this books sings its ancient song in the cadence for a modern world."
—Sarah Blackman, author of *Hex*

"Achingly effective . . . stretches a now-stodgy genre into new, magical territory. *The Poison Girl*'s braided narrative metaphorically supports stories of multigenerational and 'found' female family, proving there are many tools besides the confessional that can peel the onion of life experience."
—Cris Mazza, author of *Trickle-Down Timeline*

"This book is a revelation. Not content to just update Hawthorne's 'Rappaccini's Daughter,' Manizza Roszak refracts that story's concerns about what can and cannot be controlled—filially, botanically—across nearly a century of New York life. *The Poison Girl* guides the legacy of the American Gothic into exciting new territory."
—Kevin Allardice, author of *Any Resemblance to Actual Persons*

"A wonderfully entertaining, beautifully written novel about the dangers of being truly close to another person and the ways in which we can both hurt and heal each other.... I will be thinking about these characters for a long time to come."
—Becky Hagenston, author of *The Age of Discovery and Other Stories*

THE POISON GIRL

THE POISON GIRL

SUZANNE MANIZZA ROSZAK

spuytenduyvil

Cover image: "Conium Maculatum" from *Köhler's Medizinal-Pflanzen* by Hermann Adolph Köhler, Wilhelm Walter Müller, and Carl Friedrich Schmidt (Gera-Untermhaus: Verlag Franz Eugen Köhler, 1887-1898)

Cover and book design: Jonny Roszak

Published by Spuyten Duyvil
223 Bedford Avenue
PMB #725
Brooklyn, NY 11211

www.spuytenduyvil.net

ISBN 978-1-963908-39-8

Library of Congress Control Number: 2024945910

For my family, both present and past

Yet Giovanni's fancy must have grown
morbid while he looked down into the
garden; for the impression which the fair
stranger made upon him was as if here
were another flower, the human sister of
those vegetable ones, as beautiful as they,
more beautiful than the richest of them,
but still to be touched only with a glove,
nor to be approached without a mask.

–NATHANIEL HAWTHORNE,
"Rappaccini's Daughter" (1844)

MULBERRY

Mari Rappa

Let me explain to you our mythology of the dutiful girl. Born inevitably in New York, the girl has a father who repairs brick and limestone laid at the bottoms of small buildings and a mother who is tired, tired from the work of keeping in line the boy children she expects to and does give birth to, their little bodies ever careening up the street, the worn areas at the seams of their socks and shirts never ceasing to upset her. The girl, being conceived as a sort of afterthought and ushered into all this mess, is expected early to become something useful. Her mother as a teenager cleaned other people's houses in parts of the city where the idea of a house wasn't unheard of, transfixed by the sound of her own shoes clacking blasphemous in the hall. Anticipated for the girl is a more glorious vocation, the smooth coolness of a typewriter's keys beneath her fingers, which she will hate for the graceless way their knuckles protrude and interrupt the slim hollow of each successive bone. The girl turns out to be especially dutiful in loathing the parts of herself that offend. She grows up too short, in summer too dark, her arms and legs more than sprinkled with thick hairs that she obliterates with a razor in the early light of the bath, reusing the same blade until it is rust-brown and catches and she cuts herself, a stinging trickle of blood decorating the backside of her ankle. Before the typewriter calls she works at wrangling her older and her younger brothers into position at dinner, the biggest of them lounging at her father's elbow in an undershirt. The girl knows the anatomy of the dinner's centerpiece from top to bottom, how it begins with squished lumps of garlic and ends in a torrent of dried herbs. The bottles are constant and obliging and cheap. The girl never gets so tired that her head slumps down over her plate, remnants of sauce dotting her cheek as the rest of the family continues on, tranquilly chatting. The girl is unassailable except in dreams, where she sleeps and sleeps and wakes to discover that years have passed and wanders bewildered through an altered world until the sounds of the just-alive street below their apartment rouse her and she wakes again, for real this time, to discover that absolutely everything remains the same. She proves a delight to her parents and her brothers and to the neighbors that pass, murmuring, identifying her for the sweet thing that she is. It is useful, having a girl like her to claim as theirs. The alternatives are dangerous and for the family carry the grim possibility of dishonor, so it is a shame that this girl was not my mother and is unlikely ever to be me.

PART 1: 1937-1988

THE GRAPE EATERS

Pina Rappa

Arriving, they didn't think that this would last. Dead birds and discarded newspaper cluttering the street, crowds of people on the platform underground, the rumble of the invisible train. Like it was water about to burst from a pipe and sweep them with it into the second mouth of the tunnel.

They were named Rappa then, and Rappa was what they would call themselves until their bodies were carted away. But the adolescent husband was rechristened Jimmy, his given name more vulnerable to being sucked in and spat out transformed. He was short and slight and serious, and the name was too casual for him although in its original form it had sounded like joking in English, like he should be suited to having fun. This was fine; the country was on the cusp of something violent and brutal that they might be blamed for, and it was better to be able to disappear from view. His wife Pina was sixteen and faded daily into the chemical haze of the checkered foyers and back staircases she cleaned. All the places that wanted scouring were bleak in their winter dawns. The curtains stayed shut, blue-black with shadow, and she bent and folded herself into an unobtrusive shape and scrubbed. Her employers were people who liked their quiet, who liked to think of themselves as being alone. One eastside house hadn't changed in the decades since its four stories were raised for a single family, children propelling the elevator up from the cellar through the belly of the hall and past the cluster of sprawling bedrooms to end in the attic, where at noon the walls were a blazing white like snow. The husband would return home to their own small place craving anidduzzi, anidduzzi; she sang the word in her head. The tiny pastine drowning in broth.

Leaned against the stove the wife would listen as her spoons and colander talked to her, producing a noise that was alien even to the woman living opposite, who was not from the island the size of Massachusetts where the couple had been born. It was difficult to clean the yellowed toilets and the grout between the black and white configurations of tiles, whose owners seemed consumed by the gleaming, impossible specters of the floors and fixtures, their magnetic former paleness. As Pina had become more familiar to them, the owners had started acknowledging her presence with benevolent bursts of conversation, saying things like "Be sure to dust underneath the bottoms of the drapes!" and "Are you sure that mop has been thoroughly disinfected?" and "You can go home now, Josie. After all, it's Christmas, and you're part of the family." She preferred to talk to the bubbling and steaming pot, which made more sense and reminded her of childhood, of being ill and bowing her head into vapor.

Her least favorite of the houses had a master bedroom with a dedicated shoe closet that was almost the size of the couple's apartment. The closet was fitted with shelves and moldings that needed going over with a clump of feathers on a wooden pole, and as she entered to clean it for the eleventh time, she saw and smelled the pairs of laced and buckled women's heels and felt sick. Their shades of powder blue and cherry and drab dove gray swam blurrily as they stank. The shoe leather had been harvested from the carcasses of baby cattle. The family was absent; their live-in butler was at the market buying quail. Maybe she wouldn't work for them any longer. Kneeling on the plush carpet, she wondered what she would say to the adolescent husband, who also went on schedule to his various places of employment, his movements organized by the supervising mason, but who struck her as secretly capricious. Like any day he might just decide to remain home, on a kind of domestic strike, reading.

*

The husband was learning to read and write in English because the Rappas aspired to a parade of assimilated children, the extravagance of their ambitions surprising no one except the person who would have had to birth them. Pina had left her own mother on the island because her mother was dead and her mother's body lay untransportable in the underground spot beside a nameless infant. Once that body had been a careening blur in the bright space of someone else's field. Pina was nearsighted and had experienced the borders of her mother's moving limbs as amorphous, so that they'd bled together with the endless clusters of vines and the baskets and the women's hair beneath them covered with cloth. Rappa: *cluster, bunch*, the dictionary of American names would someday say. Was it incomprehensible or inevitable, her obsession with the idea of pregnancy? On Mulberry Street she ate grapes with pastina, boiled them into jams and infusions for tea. She peeled their skins away with a little knife, running the curved blade over the yellow edges of their flesh. She sucked the juice from their insides. She anticipated the sublime agony of labor, operating with an enthusiasm that could only belong to someone who had never experienced it. She began to forget that she had also lain with her mother in her bed, had felt her heart beat and not beat. Her mother had had five living daughters.

October 11, the Rappa boy wrote in lettering that looked machine-printed. *Today my wife is hungry. Her dinner is cooking on the stove. I filled the heavy pot with water.* As he continued on he adorned his sentences with prepositions and adjectives, gave them varied beginnings, made them longer and then shorter. It was winter again when the husband returned home with mortar under his nails and found his wife collapsed on the bathroom's patch of bare tile.

Pina's first pregnancy had taken so long to achieve that no one they knew expected her to survive it, the building's widows and matrons whispering audibly about her behind their hands. "Look at what she eats," they lamented, enjoying themselves a little too much.

"Grapes, grapes, nothing but grapes—and pastina."

None of the gesticulating spectators considered the possibility that the girl's work had had anything to do with her persistent slimness. What they did do was gossip about the smell that had started to waft around her as she passed them on the front steps and moved through the doorway toward the stairwell and the couple's fourth-floor walkup. "She stinks like an oil man's house. Like his fancy chemicals." They complained in an assortment of dialects. She would bring misfortune on their bedraggled cluster of apartments, showing up like that even at mass, smelling that way.

Seeing Pina on the floor the boy felt faint, and he tried and failed to take in the fuller landscape of her disarrayed body. She had made the housedress herself. Its sleeve was torn at the shoulder; it had caught on the doorknob on its way down. The fabric he couldn't name was marbled wet. He gathered up her hands with aberrant tenderness. They smelled as always like ammonia, like sweetly putrid fruit.

*

This went on for years. Rising up and collapsing over and over, the repeatedly miscarrying wife came to rest in increasingly creative locations. Across the sweat-sticky plastic of their only couch, which was really a loveseat and which they protected with fastidious care, her frame garish against the cheap upholstery. On the floor below the oven's grab bar, where the hanging dishtowel shielded her face from a half-luminous ceiling. The single fan whirred, filling up the hours before the husband would discover her in her familiar state. The smell continued to follow her from doorway to stairwell to foyer, although she was relieved to notice that it faded in the open air.

Mornings before the train and the string of houses, Pina would open her mouth to chew and would swallow mechanically, consuming the small fruits in whole bunches. She ate and had the sensation of feeding within her belly a resistive army of babies, ones whose hungry bodies refused to emerge separate from her blood and skin. They appreciated the tartness of the grapes, the crunching sound that echoed as she bit through their seeded cores. They accompanied her in carrying on as usual when her husband surrendered their radio to the police. It was important to do something: to prove whose side they were on. The rain emptied in angry bucketfuls onto the building's flat roof. Her feet tapped with it in time.

Once she disappeared from the street where they lived and failed to materialize in an employer's antique parlor, and the dust sat for two days together in a manner that upset its observers, who swirled their fingers in it and wondered. She didn't love the jerking subterranean pilgrimage to Coney Island, but she had promised the little grape eaters a holiday from the chemical vapors and the sloshing of the gray water in the bucket that she hauled from room to room. She climbed the stairs at the terminal station, which was older than she was and which looked it, and came face to face with salt air. There was a coast she remembered. She closed her eyes, invited its image and its smell to descend.

The pilgrimages were something that would continue unchanging once they started. It's not that the details were unaltered, only that their substance was, whether she rode in a cart on Mermaid Avenue or stood in line at Nathan's for a pineapple soda because hotdogs remained a far-off luxury or stood beneath the large and alarming image of a reclining blonde, her swimsuit squeezing her torso into a strangled shape, arms and legs burned from the sun. By now they had, improbably, one graspable child: a bundle left in the care of a neighbor to take up increasing space. "Go to work, Pina," the neighbor had commanded. The little grape eaters were her real infants and they talked to her like her mother and like the pot boiling on the stove.

It was raining again on the day when she stripped herself of clothing on the beach with the coaster rattling above it. It had never occurred to her to swim in the water beyond the boardwalk and the sand where the recumbent blondes thrust out their hips and smiled over their shoulders at each camera. But she loved and wanted to treat them, the real infants. She loved their undetectable bodies as she floated and sank and resurfaced. Every submersion lasted longer; her lungs began to hurt.

*

Telling herself she wasn't heartless, Pina never failed to return to the apartment, to her now-graying husband and their pattering boy. This also meant returning to the plastic bucket and the tall house and the others like it, whose owners were starting to dress according to a mod aesthetic. Soon lemon plaid and burnt orange corduroy would litter their tufted armchairs and the pillowy expanses of their beds. Pina's head throbbed from the smell of the polished floors and she dismissed this, but she couldn't dismiss the sounds. "Do you hear them?" she asked and asked her spouse. "Do you hear them, too?" She knew the noise existed only metaphysically, but the phrases that rose like ghost-balloons above her deserved better than an audience of one. She hoped that by some act of grace they might become audible in the dark of their kitchen, where the fainting spells had most often happened. The memory of the spells themselves no longer injured her. Between the little grape eaters and the one boy, who at seven preferred a bite of cannolo, she had managed to produce enough children.

The now-graying husband continued to covet the procession of small living faces, and he felt himself hurt by the lack of them. He wanted above all things a daughter. He felt, in fact, that this was what he was owed. The husband petitioned nightly for the restoration of justice, muttering appeals that proved typical in how they privileged the wished-for child over the health of the mother she would have if born. He wore spots on the floorboards with the spells he cast. In the cold months his fingers grew numb from counting beads. He sniffed at his wife in their bed, wondering what part of her was so intent on betraying him. He forgot to teach his firstborn to read, although he remembered to instruct the neighbor to pepper the boy with questions when he came back from school. "Go to work, Mino," she told him.

We've all heard the excuses: the small man didn't mean Pina any unkindness. His intentions didn't matter; she grew sallow and listless after collapsing in the shoe closet of the house she'd never resigned from cleaning, her legs in this instance giving way not to herald a doomed pregnancy but because her blood vessels were vasodilating, relaxed by a recognizable constellation of hormones. This time it was the two perfect children of the house's new owner who found her lying beside the ascending rows of block and kitten heels.

"But mother!" the girl cried. "You'll never guess what she's done!"

She was staring in horror at the supple left boot that had been knocked from the shelf and which the fainting maid was now using as a pillow. The go-go boot was still a year away from being invented, but wearing Yves Saint Laurent was already supposed to be a shortcut to joy and abundance. The maid's error was accidental but couldn't be forgiven.

They discharged her that same day, although she still had the rotation of other fashionable houses to fall back on and for a while did just that, drinking condensed soup from a thermos as she scrubbed to keep from throwing up. Yes, she was unhappy in the condition that the husband who was no longer a boy had wished her into. Her cheekbones, drained of color, gave the impression of being uncomfortable in her face. The little grape eaters were inside her with a sibling; they were there and they were talking and they were ravenous. Before long she would retire from the jobs she still had. The firstborn would watch her, concerned, waiting as usual for Easter or a birthday, for some happy planned event.

*

The expectant wife rattled in bed like a heavy shell, a treasure dragged in from the neighboring beach. Confined there Pina was tired of the noise, its pace and pitches. The owners of the tall house never saw her again.

For them it was not a substantial loss—they hired somebody else. The chemical haze continued to circulate, making its way through the politely interconnected rooms.

RICOTTA

Luca Rappa

I was nine on the day our mother died. What I mean is that it was my first day of being really nine, the day after my birthday, and it was also the beginning of my being half an orphan. Looking back I'm able to see a satisfying symmetry in the universe's method of organizing these events of my life. In nine more years I would be legally emancipated without the approval of a judge and would plot to shake off home and become untraceable by a father I hoped not to see again. That I also had a sister who was faultless in this was something regrettable and something I could do nothing about. She had been blameless in our mother's death, too—I believed that even though the event so closely followed her birth that a less scientific response to their correlation might have led me to a different idea—and yet the shape of her long childhood was going to be unmistakably different because of our family tragedy, and like my leaving her behind, this was an unavoidable outcome of the way things were.

The sounds of my birthday were not the ones I had been dreaming about for months. Now that I was at school I spent only a third of my day in the apartment across the hall from where we slept, but the hours there stretched on like the hours in the brick building with the wide windows where I walked myself in the morning and sat almost without moving, taking in the hum of the teacher's voice and the suggestions of voices muffled by the walls of other classrooms and the uncomfortable feeling of the wooden chair pressing my pants against my skin. My father had dressed me and then expected me to dress myself in a shirt that closed with buttons and in slacks whose fabric bunched in voluminous folds as I slid myself into the space between the desk and seat. I was a cheap imitation of an American office manager, which in his view was preferable to my looking as though I was going to be spending the bulk of my adult years laying and relaying bricks. I had a few friends, and their parents weren't bothered by the prospect of their children's initiation into various familiar and expected professions. They distrusted our teachers and became irritated when they had to encounter the pretensions of formally educated people. For us this is an old and unsurprising story. My father, however, spent his hunched nights examining the pages of second-hand magazine issues, flipping with a regular rhythm from glossy column to worn translation dictionary and back again, and in this way he learned about "The Origin of Speech" and "The 600-Foot Radio Telescope" and the killer insects that would paralyze and dissolve the insides of their prey before living on them for days or maybe weeks. He didn't realize that in the apartment across the hall I sat mesmerized by the television instead of studying while he was gone, or that sometimes I spent hours cutting snowflakes out of thin white paper with a pair of kitchen shears as a rerun Marvin Miller began to address his audience. "John Beresford Tipton, a fabulously wealthy and fascinating man, whose many hobbies included his habit of giving away one million dollars—"

As my father pored over *Scientific American* my mother sat dreaming or slept early, and it was my mother's rarer sounds that I wanted to hear on the anniversary of her giving birth to me. It was possible that we would take the day off. It was possible that I would open my eyes in the late morning to see the back of my mother's blue housedress and hear her whipping soft cheese in a bowl. My bed was in the living room and the living room was open to the kitchen, so it was not unreasonable of me to imagine this. But my mother was pregnant again and destined for bed rest, an uncomfortable novelty for someone whose registered occupation was "house cleaner" in the U.S. census, and even if she hadn't been expected to lay quiet and obedient she was not going to be available to bake for me. Because it happened that my sister would burst from our mother's body with unanticipated speed: a month early and two hours after I had wiped the floor clean with a rag, sopping up the lake of barely yellow fluid she'd been sloshing inside of, which had ended up puddling there because our mother was up and walking although they had said she should not be. I was still eight; my own birth had taken place at night instead of noon.

*

Did you know that a woman who has experienced the loss of a pregnancy is twice as likely to die in labor or in its wake? Today I wonder how that figure might be compounded when the losses pile up like unattended laundry in the corner of a dingy room. We buried our mother in a graveyard in one of the outer boroughs because the cemetery on our street had long been full. By then a century's worth of poor immigrant bodies had been ferried across the East River at 10th Street or had been otherwise transported from the city to the flat green spaces between the small deciduous and evergreen trees. We buried our mother, and again I say *our mother* because my sister had survived the events of the previous four days and was with us, wrapped up in a blanket that was green and yellow because the neighbor woman who watched me and expected to watch my sister, too, hadn't known whether she would be another boy or a girl. Our father had named her Beatrice and bound her tightly so that her arms were at her sides and couldn't flail. I was the one who held her at the gravesite and the one who started to call her Bice—Bice because she didn't need to speak for god, because I already wanted her not to be the object of some man's gaze from far away.

I returned to school. Bice remained in our building while our father continued at work like nothing had happened. She was small, and one of her eyes was a mottled brown-blue and not the other's muddy green. Despite having been premature she seemed no different from the babies I'd seen wheeled into church or rocked on the building's squat front stoop, and she didn't need the intensive care that we couldn't have gotten her, instead surviving fine on evaporated milk and corn syrup before beginning the same bland diet of pastina that our mother had fed me and our neighbor had taught me to name: stelline, anellini. We boiled the hard shapes in water in the early mornings before my sister went to the apartment across the way. It was easy for me to guess what species of entertainments awaited her. The buzz of the television, the snip-snip of the kitchen shears.

The neighbor woman was getting older and more apocalyptic in her beliefs, so she wasn't troubled by our father's decision that Bice, whose home birth had never been reported to the city's department of public health, would not be joining me in the brick building with the wide windows. My sister grew slowly taller as her caretaker rotated between the old reruns of *The Millionaire* and a family copy of *La Sacra Bibbia*, whose references to beasts and monsters and darkness were the ones the woman favored. "Apparve ancora un altro segno nel cielo," she recited, "ed ecco un gran dragone rosso, che avea sette teste, e dieci corna; e in su le sue teste v'erano sette diademi." *Yet another sign appeared in the sky: here was a great red dragon with seven heads and ten horns, and on its heads seven coronets.* Bice repeated the grammatically outmoded sentences when we were together late at night, murmuring at first awake and then in sleep, until I could say them from memory like she did. The great dragon, the primeval serpent. I was old enough to amuse myself around the city after school let out, and I had started avoiding the apartment whose windows overlooked the sidewalk where I'd ridden my bicycle in ornate loops to evade passersby. The neighbor spoke to almost no one anyway—she had never been as social as the other women, and I think she lived on the allowance our father gave her—so she had no trouble not telling stories up and down the block about the little girl with the bewitching eye.

At dinner our father reclaimed the task of feeding Bice with a doggedness and a jealousy I couldn't explain. He spoke sweetly to her as he held the spoon, saying "Mancia, mancia, figghia mia," and he fed her that way even when she was five and six and seven years old, taking the spotted stem of the utensil between his fingers as he prepared to stuff her mouth with large bites of whatever we were eating. Then one night I came home unexpectedly soon after a shift at the bookstore where I had gotten a part-time job and found my sister wailing, our father looming over her, his free hand shaking her arm.

"I want you to eat!" He was shouting in an intermittently emphatic English. "Don't *argue* with me!"

Bice's face maintained its crumpled position as I watched from the apartment doorway that interrupted our excuse for a parlor. Later what I would recall was her brows and lips, the tiny soundless adjustments they made as she cried. I would envision crossing the narrow room and wrestling the spoon from our father's hand. I would imagine raising my voice. *You're hurting her.* Instead our father somehow never turned his head to see me and neither did my sister and I took advantage of this, wheeling back around and closing the door behind me before they could notice I'd been there—which is to say that I actually believed they hadn't. I returned to the bookstore, which had once been located next door to the headquarters of the American Bible Society and would eventually become the setting of a Woody Allen movie. I had a key and I let myself in and walked the darkened aisles to the stockroom at the back of the shop, where I curled up and slept on the floor. I was the age our mother had been the year she and our father had first arrived in New York. Our father and his will.

*

I have no idea how the rumors started about Bice and our mother, but soon a girl I liked but never talked to approached me in the hallway between classes, her eyes glinting. Was it true that my mother had been poisoned by one of the filthy rich businesspeople whose houses she had cleaned? Was it true that I had a sister whose very existence my father was hiding from the neighborhood because she was possessed, haunted by the spirits of the dozen babies my mother was said to have miscarried? The girl wasn't interested in me or my sequestered sister or our dead mother as anything but a gothic spectacle, and I hated her until I had made it out of the building and down the block: until I was kicking at the garbage cans whose faces decorated the corner where I considered crossing against the signal because I couldn't stand my unmoving body.

Bice was still under the care of our neighbor and was barely let out of doors, but she'd taken to standing at the window in the afternoon sun and would watch the women passing below her as intently as if they were her friends. I understood her well enough to be able to say which of the strolling and chatting forms would catch her attention: the younger ones in bright one-shoulder tops and the older ones in shirtdresses and cardigans, thick bracelets overburdening their wrists. The men she couldn't be bothered with; what mattered was who she wanted to turn into. Had someone who'd seen her behind the glass taken the time to notice our family resemblance? She never opened the apartment door for strangers. It had seemed easy for our father to convince her to keep herself hidden, capitalizing on the stories of devil-beasts that would someday walk the city uncloaked as they now walked everywhere people appeared to be. He had always been selectively religious. At our Church of the Most Precious Blood, the parish priest would raise an eyebrow as our father thumbed conspicuously through a magazine, unmoved by the deeper implications of the archways and the tall pillars he had brought me to observe. "Look at the mottled color of the stone," he would say. "Look how they've polished it." He would say this because for all his talk of white-collar life he maintained a love of building, of creation. Then he would continue reading about the Green Flash or about nitrogen mustards or the physiology of breath. Then he would return to the apartment to repeat for Bice a homily that was actually of his own composition, one populated with the nightmares that would keep her home.

*

I had already decided I was not a hero when, on my days off from the bookstore uptown, the senior boys began following me from the high school to our front door. At first their game was harmless enough; they made vaguely menacing gestures toward me and I walked quickly and then ran or ducked into an alley where I lay under an illegally parked car or climbed into a dumpster. It seemed normal, like an unwritten requirement we all had to complete for graduation.

Things escalated on the afternoon when they started yelling insults after me as I fled. "So," cried one of them, "I hear you've got someone to clean your house after all!"

"Yeah, Pete," another taunted. "How come your shirts always stink?"

"You smell like burnt plastic," a third boy offered.

"Are those mortar stains?"

Pete was not my name. I walked faster.

"Maybe it's because your sister only has one eye."

"That's it, guys—she just can't see!" The three of them were chuckling and high-fiving each other as they accelerated behind me. "We ought to be nicer. We ought—pay her—visit." Now I was running and they were, too, and there were little gaps in their speech where words should have been.

We had reached the shallow stoop of the building with its few steps, and I felt myself careening forward. The steps were empty of the mothers and their babies and there was no one to break my fall. It was natural that I would lose consciousness and wake up disoriented in my bed in the living room, our father's hand heavy on my chest as it rose and fell. What made less sense was the sequence of events that some of the building's other women tenants would recall having witnessed from their own street-facing windows. "But she looked so young," they murmured. Dark like their daughters but with too short a dress, its seams pulling apart at the armpits. One of the boys had convulsed and fallen down on the sidewalk. Another had doubled over and vomited, the vomit laced with blood, the blood a blossoming pink against the concrete. A third, the one with the taste for bad similes, was in the hospital. It was unclear whether he would survive. No one had seen my sister do anything criminal. She had opened the door to the building; she had stepped outside in her bare feet. She was almost eight; I was still sixteen. The neighbor was chastised: she should keep a closer watch. The convulsions and the retching were determined to be a strange coincidence or perhaps an act of god.

*

One birthday followed another and our father continued feeding Bice like an infant. I wasn't surprised to see him return from the bank with the down payment for a house in Middle Village. The house is on a street that runs between two cemeteries, although neither is the one where our mother was interred, and at the time it was reachable by a train that started at Coney Island. If you fell asleep on your way back from the beach, our new neighborhood was where you would find yourself when the train jolted you awake at the other end of the line. The house had a garden in the backyard, our father told us, where my sister could run and play. Bice smiled at this news. Next to the apocalyptic stories of *La Sacra Bibbia*, she most preferred its narratives of plants and petals. "Quale è il giglio fra le spine, tale è l'amica mia fra le fanciulle," she'd once told me, like the words were a delicious secret. *As is the lily among the thorns, so is my beloved among the girls.* I thought she would enjoy staying at home while our father worked, ruling over the garden by herself. She would be happy in the unmediated sunlight, the little trees they would plant talking to her like brothers.

They piled their things into the small hired truck and I helped them, telling them I would meet them at the house on 67th Road. Then I walked purposely in the wrong direction with my one bag and took a PATH train to New Jersey. In Hoboken where I exited there was no breeze or sound once the train cars disappeared from view, and I felt inside a deadness and also an irresistible feeling of relief.

GROCERY

Margherita Caffarel

It took Margherita Caffarel a decade to miss the girl or to admit that she did. Bey-ah-TREE-chay, named for the joy she was expected to bring as if that were not a stale and risky method of wishmaking, as if the reason for the neighbor's role as bambinaia wasn't that the girl was half an orphan from almost her moment of birth. Half-orphans—that was what her brother had called them, as in *I'm half an orphan; who cares whether I run into the path of an oncoming car?* Yes, who?

Actually Margherita was not so old: she had been thirty-nine when the brother was born, and her hair was taking its time in whitening although her skin itched with a crawling feeling that she feared she had because she should have been birthing babies and she wasn't doing so, had little expectation of seeing her body bloated and spoiled and full. Margherita lived alone, and the children and the other women in the building were not from the town from which her family had emerged after generations of bathing in the same one river.

The streets of the town had been quiet, lined with three-story houses and trees that reached as high, some of which were green in winter and would collect snow and birds equally. As a child Margherita would have preferred to stay, not caring that the reason her parents and her parents' parents had made the town their home was a threat of death that, as they had followed the river, had followed them for an untold number of years. They had belonged to the wrong religious sect; they rejected purgatory and indulgences. There were plenty among their ancestors who for these heresies had been burned or torn limb from limb and then hurled from cliffs. Rumor had it that these martyrs had been more than willing to be made an example of; their killers hailed from a church that they equated with le abbominazioni della terra. *The abominations of the earth*, made to sound explosive by Diodati's double-b. The rest of them had been more practical and had done their best to flee and settle into the array of mountain hamlets, remaining there until several generations had been born and died and the living adults found it prudent to start over again, on a different continent altogether.

*

The post-traumatic consequences of repeated escape left Margherita and her family sweating in the evenings between their sheets and blankets, and maybe that was why it was so easy for her to believe in the saddest potentialities for even their newer life. When permitted she roamed the American city to which her parents had now brought her, and the sights she saw that stuck were the revelatory ones. Women on the corner cried and held their children, girls smaller than she was who stared as a stranger took photographs instead of helping, keeping his distance so that what would last, what was really immortalized was the journalist and the sea of useless strolling bystanders, their gabardine pants and blank faces.

Seeing this the neighbor thought from early on that the world would end, and she wanted to be helpful and also found it pointless, and this contradictory understanding of her situation made it foreseeable that as a caretaker of children she would be both kind and cold. The strangeness of the children's father was their fate and not her business. She heard him yell in the evenings and kept to herself and her crocheting or her book. But she would watch the children and make sure they didn't electrocute or drown themselves while their father was pointing bricks, and on occasion she would hug them although neither seemed to like it, the boy squirming away and the girl's body freezing when Margherita had thought the girl would melt with relief.

Done attempting to be motherly, she would turn on the television or would read from that bible translated by a man born in exile. It was mostly the girl, Béa, who gained exposure to Diodati's verse. She called her Béa because her one blue eye looked like the skies of the place the neighbor had come from and in that place their names had sometimes originated across the border. Margherita looked the girl in the face and saw tree branches turned to icicles against an expanse of almost cobalt. Then she was homesick and she forgot her age and felt that she and Béa were two children. She needed the book to distract them; it was a less dangerous thing although it also spoke of calamities. The pair of them read, and the arcane text was a labyrinth that unfurled in front of them until the girl believed its words and so did her caretaker, more than she had before.

*

The apartment was already a hermitage, cramped and remote from the street because of the number of flights they had to climb to reach it and the window sashes that refused to budge. As a child Margherita had lived here with her parents; now that their bodies were buried in

Queens she was the one tenant left in 4A. "Why don't they open?" the girl had asked, pointing toward the windows. The neighbor couldn't tell her. She started going out less and less. The boy left groceries at her door, packets and cans so begrudgingly fetched from the Grand Superette that he never wanted to admit he had brought them.

One day it was cold and there was snow outside like there would have been in the mountain town. Margherita opened the door to the bathroom, where she had been sitting on the toilet with a hand mirror passed down from a childless aunt—a gift that for the longest time she had been afraid to examine because she suspected that the reflection she'd find there would be the aunt's and not her own—and on crossing into the hallway she saw the boy's sister on the floor among the fragments of a broken jar of canned and oozing fruit. She hadn't heard the glass break and yet there were translucent shards strewn around the girl and across the trough that her woolen skirt made as she sat, and along her low cheekbones she had wiped traces of this jumble of red.

It was a mess that would have to be cleaned, food to replace for no good reason.

"What did you do?" Margherita bellowed.

Béa didn't flinch. She looked up and past the neighbor, unperturbed, her face expressionless. That was when Margherita became convinced that Béa was either a saint she would refuse to worship or a child haunted. She backed away from the image that the girl's frame made against the floor. She went to the closet for the dustpan and brush and to the sink for a sponge. Béa sat motionless as the neighbor swept up the glass, as she wiped the juice from the wood.

*

Did they shut the girl in with Our Lady of Pompeii or The Little

Sisters of the Assumption or Our Mother of Perpetual Help? The monastery and its cloisters border a river. The girl's family moved; Margherita washed her hands of them. She tried to forget the girl, the name she'd called her. At night she sweated and dreamed of disaster, the nearby flapping of wings.

BUNDT CAKE

Trudy Whitehall

From the first you could see that the new arrivals were strange, that they wouldn't be acceptable. All you had to do was look. Look to see the girl wearing her threadbare jumper, dragging along the sidewalk beside the house a clear plastic sack, a sack like one you'd place trash into at a construction site, and the sack itself populated with a few plushly fake animals and what appeared from my window to be other badly darned dresses and skirts and maybe a sweater, a sweater because past winters could be depended on to be cold but this was the same reason she should have had more of them with her than she did, and then the girl again staring down at the asphalt as she carried a piece of men's luggage across and up the road from the truck that was double-parked in front of our stoop. That's right, she was staring down the cracks in the pavement and the sidewalk that were filled with weeds, not looking ahead toward the picture window of the newly purchased home which I can assure you leans jauntily out from its pea-green siding, toward the tiny cheerful awning that adorns the doorway—these are features shared by all the houses in the neighborhood and we love them, are loyal to them because of what they mean we have succeeded in doing, settling here, every year scrubbing clean the faces of our concrete and our brick front steps and the bulkheads that give way to industrious basements where our husbands whittle forest creatures for our many children out of wood, solder together pieces of colored glass into flat imitations of holiday candles for hanging in a bedroom window—and the girl wasn't moved by any of this but instead appeared ungrateful and despite the way I exerted myself to imagine her reasons I couldn't fathom why. Even when I knocked with a late-season bundt, its ski slopes if I may say covered immaculately with ice and dotted with the crunchiest little green and red balls, even then was I left four minutes to wait so that my hands were numb when they let me in and the man smiled with silver in his black hair but the girl's face had an expression like something sour, like she had frozen that way and couldn't move, and I thought to myself how badly raised she must have been not to have tripped laughing to the door, not to have taken the cake and my coat with it, asking me in the usual way if I wanted to sit down so I could tell her that no, I had more pies, cookies, nut-breads in the oven but I would be so happy if they would visit us for dinner some night because after all they now belonged to us. Instead I stood awkwardly in the kitchen, on the dirty linoleum, and what could have possessed her to do what she did?— when I offered just the tiniest kernel of advice about the rumples of her blouse to rather than thanking me for the gesture begin yelping as though I'd shot her, declaring that I, I was the disheveled one—oh, she didn't say it in those words but you should have seen me; my revulsion was obvious and in a hurry I gathered myself up and departed although since I am a Christian I left the baked goods. Yes, I'd observe her later in the perfunctory front yard tending the shrub they planted, the miniature tree that I think must have been a kind of shrunken cypress because of course that's what they would have chosen and I'd see her there when she should have been at school but perhaps the man had decided to undertake her education at home because I can't imagine a girl with her personality would have found much success in the happy atmosphere of P.S./I.S. 87, where we were raising jolly tykes into diligent future leaders, and I wasn't of a mind to investigate her welfare as honestly we know a family like that, a family like that is best left to itself, for the good of the neighborhood, of its name, the established order of everything.

CARVE

Bice Rappa

They occupied themselves in the ordinary ways that people do on starting again. What most amazed her during the initial drive to the town designed for averageness was the vividity of the world through which they passed: the windows of the rented truck were open, and it was one of the unseasonably warm days in a year that had also featured unseasonably cold ones, and although it was February the birds were out and she swore to her father that she could hear them over the noise of the road. The appearance of the northern cardinals and dark-eyed juncos wasn't special, he muttered from behind the wheel, having read about them in *Birding*, where he had felt himself cowed, then entranced, by the life lists of member ornithologists and laypeople who had managed to hunt down and observe six hundred North American species in a span of years, voyagers whose accomplishments had led the magazine editor to speculate that soon the faraway threshold of seven hundred species witnessed would be reached. Bice was unmoved by the recitation of these statistics. The windows of the neighboring apartment where her father had sent her instead of dispatching her to school had been screwed shut from the outside because otherwise they refused to close and because the manager of their building hadn't cared for the intricacies of the New York City housing code. Or at least that was what her father had claimed. Today she would have the possibility of touching things that he had only let her see, and she was more impressed with the sensory depth of this touchable world than with the hypotheticals of a culture of accumulation that in her view was disturbing—creepy—even if she didn't say so.

The new house was forty years an old one; after an ebullient initial decade it had lost its charm. There was brick in the kitchen, and the cabinets had that reddish stain that occupants of cabins seem to love; they popped in an eyewatering way against the olive tiles on the walls. The tiles belonged in a bathroom and suggested that the house's former owners had had some secret to cover up in their midcentury remodel of its white surfaces, something that had kept them from being contented until every inch of the plaster had been concealed. This was a row house, though, not a detached and isolated country spot, and it was hard to imagine anything happening here that exceeded the girl's everyday standards for the horrific. The most obvious violence done had been to the garden, which was fenced with chain link over wood because apparently one barrier between yards hadn't been enough. Now the garden was full of waist-high weeds and vines that almost effaced the birdbath and the overturned flowerpot the house's most recent occupants had left behind. Inside there were too many bedrooms for the size of the place, which meant that each was cramped and that Bice's expectation of relief at no longer sleeping in a living room attached to a kitchen was disappointed.

"E bonu," said Bice's father. The house had relieved them of the building manager and his despotism; she would please keep quiet about what else it was.

If the girl didn't enter the new school through its green double doors, if she didn't stand admiring or scowling at the bronzed eagle monument that stood between the front steps and the stone archway the color of spoiled cream, that didn't mean her days weren't busy. She spent her first mornings in the new-old house refolding her father's work pants and undershirts and her own crinkled dresses, placing them into a succession of color-coordinated piles. They didn't have the furniture to fill the tiny spare bedroom that he would claim as a study for stacking his magazines or the even smaller one downstairs that they would employ as a den, absorbing Friday installments of *Circle of Fear* in the weeks before the show was canceled, her father scoffing from the plastic-covered loveseat where her pregnant mother used to faint. Knowing this, Bice decided to use a dresser as their new TV stand and the former kitchen table as her father's desk; for now they could eat their meals on folding trays. The actual shuffling of the furniture from room to room would happen later, a neighbor man's hands moving in time with the gray-stained ones she knew because the pieces were heavy and they hadn't planned this layout before moving in. The neighbor who returned to the house to help her father a second time was a newer arrival on the block. Like them, he had lived beforehand in an apartment somewhere in the cacophonous space between Broome and Canal. "One—two—three!" the men cried in different languages as they prepared for the weight of the wood. From the landing Bice watched them move down the stairs, her father hunched like a snail over the bureau's smooth top.

The thing about the house that most puzzled her was the speed with which dust and hair and other debris collected there: in the corners of rooms, the one bathtub, the crevices of the plain moldings that made their way around the doors and windows. She would run a finger over the banister and find it covered with a smooth coating of fur, would rummage through the cabinet under the sink for a rag and a can of Pine-Sol and would sweep away what she assumed was some detritus of a former house pet only to see the patch of wood blanketed the next day with another sort of filth. Something similar was happening in the back garden, which they had hoed and cleared of invasive plants and redone with a combination of recognizable vegetables, flowers, and other leafy species whose names Bice didn't know. Her father had sent away for the seeds, ordering them out of a newsprint catalog, and had insisted on planting them himself. She hid in her room on the day he saw that the weeds once more were overtaking the wanted blossoms and their companions. The sounds of his expletives overlapped and echoed; they were one little explosion and then another.

Always obsessive about her eating, he began placing larger and larger plates of chicken and potatoes in front of her, the chicken being an item they could now afford and the potatoes being a late-stage concession to American habits. She would eat until her abdomen and her chest ached and he would lean back in his chair, looking less troubled, as though he believed that if he could make her grow faster than the ecosystem of the house and garden could replenish itself then he would somehow win his war with both. He wouldn't let her touch the food while he prepared it; her mere presence in the room was unacceptable. She would let him spoil her, he said. She grew as used to the ache as it was possible to be.

*

Invariably there was dust on the girl's clothes when she went to the butcher. At first she had visited the shop at noon so that he wouldn't know she hadn't been at school. Then it was summer and the timing no longer mattered.

"Whose turn is it?" he'd ask, winking like an old man although he was only seventeen, and she would jump and turn to look.

Yes, it was just her waiting. "Mine, I think."

"Okay, bambina, and what will you have?"

The butcher was not from her parents' small island or from the larger country to which it had been appended, and he spit the word out with an exaggerated cadence, with vowels that turned it unintentionally ugly.

"Two chicken breasts and a steak, please."

"One steak?"

"Just one."

The steak was for Bice's father. More and more he made himself different food than the dishes he laid out for her, or else he asked her to cook him a single slab of meat for practice. She didn't care to eat the steak anyway; the redness of the meat was worrisome. The butcher cut steadily through the marbled flesh. The butcher's apron was tinged with red; his fingers were stained the way her father's were with mortar. In the window were the carcasses of more dead animals, animals that still had hooves although they hung from hooks. Somewhere another butcher was holding a whole pig in his arms, reaching out its paw to a smiling customer for an advertisement. Somewhere a man was crouching in front of the glass, painting the word BEEF in aggressive white lettering. The room swam with red, like she was looking through tinted cellophane. She dug into the pockets of her skirt for the fistful of coins the butcher wanted. *Now is the time to restock your freezer*, the newspaper ads declared, but they never bought their food in bulk. She did this almost daily and always it was the same blood, the same heat and vertigo.

Over time she sensed that it was better not to resist the strange rhythms of the house. On spring afternoons she had stretched herself out in the dirt of the garden, face down or bared to the sky, which more often than not had been dark with an impending rain. The weatherman had delighted in announcing the unusualness of the weather: it hadn't rained so much in May since 1888. He had savored the near-rhyming endings of that month and year. Now it was October, and instead of scouring the house's rooms their cleaner lay clothed in the empty bathtub. Feeling the dust bunnies under her hands and elbows and feet, Bice discovered that she favored the feathery remnants of skin and bugs and pollen over their absence. Now it was her father's turn to be disturbed. He remarked on the disordered state of her wardrobe, entreated her to act more like a reanimated version of her mother. She listened to him less and less; she was ten and was becoming capable of ignoring him.

Where they agreed was in the matter of the garden plants themselves, which the younger Rappa child had been instructed to tend while her father was away, and which she was happy to water and pat and talk to because although she didn't mind the weeds she loved the blossoms. There was the flower that looked like Queen Anne's lace, the verdant leaf with its shiny black berries, the bush that branched into delicate clusters of white petals, its thicker stalks ever shooting off to produce new and more slender segments crowned with the pale crocheted balls. For as long as she could remember Bice's cheeks had been redder than the average girl's—she knew this from looking in the mirror and then out the window at the people who passed under it—and sometimes little bumps or streaks like scratches appeared on her hands when she had been in the backyard for too long. She wondered whether she had grown allergic to the sun from her time indoors. "What's this, pà?" she would demand to know when her father stepped through the door and into the dining alcove where they'd finally placed a compact round table with two hidden leaves.

"Again?" He would smile, leaning toward her to inspect the blotch. Then he would back away quickly and head to his study for the Merck manual, which sat most often between the towering piled issues of *Scientific American* and now *Weatherwise* and *Mercury*. He would sink into a repurposed dining chair, savoring the opportunity to leaf through the bound book before reemerging to placate her. Only the diction of his responses varied: "It's nothing." "It's normal." "Don't worry; it should disappear by morning." "There, there—you look tired. Figghia mia, figghia mia." Her hands were streaked like the butcher's. The lines and bumps dissipated with increasing speed until they no longer appeared at all. Bice's father told her not to tend the vegetables anymore, that he wanted her to relax and enjoy the rest of the garden.

"You're my lily among the thorns," he said, borrowing the syntax of *La Sacra Bibbia*.

*

When the birds descended she was standing on the square of front lawn next to the rusted bulkhead, having just pampered with hose water the baby cypress that they'd planted for privacy. The hose was covered with a film like the one that blanketed the furniture inside, and she was clapping her hands less to shake the dust from her fingers than because she liked the sound. Then the rhythm of her clapping and its echoes against the siding of the house gave way to a less decipherable noise, a disorganized kind of beating, and she realized that her hands had stilled themselves without her meaning them to and that the noise was coming from above the rear garden.

Normally birds seemed to avoid their property, but in the minute it took her to pass through and reach the back of the house, dozens of winged creatures had alighted on the nameable vegetables and the gorgeous anonymous blooms and on the tops of the tall encroaching weeds. Seeing their bellies more than tinged with white, Bice's father would have called the birds a flutter, a crew. Their whistles to her were ominous; they made a sound that resembled the neighborhood sirens she remembered from the place where they used to live.

She began counting them: five, thirty-one, fifty-six. They watched her as she inched closer, their eyes like black beads. As she stared and they stared she became less afraid and began instead to want to capture one of them—a smaller, younger junco whose streaked feathers appealed to her. None of their people were built for being alone, and her brother was nineteen that fall and had not been heard from and this was why since they had moved it had been just her and her father in the house. She pictured her brother bent over a book that was not the northern neighbor's bible, her brother turning pages as he taught her to identify one letter after the next.

The birds stared and whistled and hopped from flower to branch, and they continued carrying on in this way even when the moon appeared. Her father came home too late for a shared dinner; through the closed door to her bedroom she heard his footsteps advance and recede. In the dark she had expected the birds to rest, and she had the impression that in avoiding sleep they were trying to warn her. Did they hope to mark the presence of some intruding threat? They did not know her father, these birds. Like the house he had his advantages; he could be depended on to protect her, whatever else he was.

*

Here was Jimmy Rappa in the study with a pair of scissors, cutting.

"Look, look—the pectoralis major," he murmured in the direction of the door. "And here the supracoracoideus. The largest muscles, for flight. Next the intestine—"

His two hands were moving, suspended in air. Outside it was morning, and the rest of the birds had fled because her father had captured and killed their companion, and their absence was something Bice felt intuitively but didn't want to see as she retraced the path from the doorway of the study to her room. Her door had no lock. Avoiding the sight of the window, she laid herself on top of the bed. It wasn't enough; she rose and knelt and crawled belly-down under its frame. She traced the letters of her name in the feathery clumps of skin and bugs and pollen. She considered carefully where they stood, what she might do.

The largest muscles, for flight.

PUDDING

Quinn O'Leary

The butcher was in a corner of the empty shop. The butcher was in a corner of the empty shop, and he was sitting and reading a novel. The novel the butcher was reading was about a bullied high schooler. The novel was about a bullied high schooler with telekinetic abilities that promised to upend with stunning permanency the rhythms of life in an average American town. The bullied high schooler in the novel was, critically, a girl. The bullied high schooler was a girl who had been made to go to church picnics and who at church picnics had found herself ridiculed for a wardrobe malfunction that threatened to expose her nakedness to the world. The malfunction would not be the first or the last time the bullied high schooler's physical self would be treated like a joke against her will. It wouldn't be the first or the last time because the novel would begin with the bullied high schooler in a compromising position in the shower and would move quickly on to a host of indignities: the peanut butter in her dark hair—always the butcher imagined her this way although this detail was inaccurate to the text itself—or the skinned knees the butcher inferred she would acquire on being tripped, falling up and down the aisles of classroom after classroom. The butcher was reading in fits and starts, sometimes the same word or sentence or passage more than once, as one customer after another pulled open the door and jangled the bell that prompted him to look up from the book whose spine he had already broken. The butcher would feel a disorienting mix of hope and annoyance at the sound of the bell; his shop was not busy and busyness was what he needed both financially and personally, but on the other hand he was occupied with the book and was anxious to discover what he felt certain would be the bullied high schooler's cunning and talented acts of vengeance. The butcher read on, and now the teenagers were screaming at their naked classmate. Now the teenagers were screaming at their naked classmate whom they showed no mercy because children—for that is what they still technically were—well, children were cruel; this was something that the butcher also knew, being the sort of young man about whom small boys would whistle and sing mean-spirited songs. The song the teenagers were directing toward their naked classmate referred to her as food. It made her a lump of dessert. The butcher read on, and as he read he envisioned the face of the classmate as the face of the neighborhood girl who shopped there for her father although he knew that unlike the novel's anti-heroine she didn't go to school. There was something unsettling about the neighborhood girl, like she might at any time prove capable of setting the shop aflame. A state of emergency would be declared. White papers would be written. The place where they lived was average; the butcher knew it and the neighborhood girl knew it and they all knew it. The butcher flipped pages he'd skimmed instead of reading. "One steak?" the butcher asked. He always asked her. Always the answer stayed the same.

GIVE ME BOLOGNA AND
GIVE ME BREAD

Bice Rappa

The earliest story I can tell begins with my father leaving me alone. I was ten and had just found him in his office dissecting the carcass of the wild bird that I had seen in the backyard and had hoped to keep as a pet. I was horrified at the dissection of the bird and at its killing, a crime of which I was sure my father was also guilty. Believing this I retreated to my room, and instead of finding and contradicting and comforting me my father let me keep to myself. He wasn't fond of displays of emotion other than his own—"Please, figghia, control yourself," he would say when I was angry about a snowstorm I had missed while sleeping or the sideways glances of an unfriendly shop assistant—and because he never thought of my affective life as his responsibility or as anything but an aberrance, it was typical of him to wait for the swirl of my emotions to settle rather than feeling called to intercede. What he didn't count on was that I was developing my own consciousness. What I didn't count on was how long it would take me to act on this in a way that would get me anywhere I wanted to go.

The previous June my father had asked if he should enroll me in school. In planning to ask this question my father had imagined himself playing an elaborate trick on a little girl. He had never allowed me to go to school before and he was not about to start now, but he expected the illusion of choice to get me on his side, to better ensconce me in the home he'd bought us. "Do you want to go to school, Bice?" he asked me and I shook my head, telling him no, realizing what he was trying to accomplish and what I was supposed to say. "No, pà," I said because I understood what a good daughter was and I had a vague sense that appearing to be one would be beneficial.

My father had spent a decade hiding the fact that I was alive, telling neighbors who asked that I had died after my mother and that the cries they heard were a figment of their imaginations or had come through the speakers of our TV. Now he belatedly registered my existence with the city and applied to homeschool me, and although the curriculum he proposed shouldn't have met the threshold of substantial equivalence that the board had set, its members approved his application anyway and he went back to work and I was given the run of the house, which wasn't at all what he had promised them. And today the bird was dead and had been cut apart; its gray feathers littered the desk.

In the face of my father's violence I had two alternatives. I could go on as if nothing had happened, drawing his attention away from the angle of revenge I was planning. I could also confront my father with the conviction I suspected I might possess, could draw myself up fierce—he was a tiny man and by some miracle of genetics I could almost look him in the eye without having to lift my chin—at which point I would have to wait and see whether I survived his reaction.

I decided to keep quiet, but at the same time I organized things so that I would go my own way, and this man who shared my blood would have no idea.

*

As I walked along in the direction of the school building, I recited in my head all the errors my father had made that had led him to deserve my lies. There were proven crimes as well as suspected ones; most obviously, he had abandoned me. I was thinking about how I had been barricaded in the new place, expected to darn my father's socks and to prepare his dinners even when he still insisted on cooking for me himself. My mother had cleaned up after untidy rich people for two decades and had then died, and instead of locating my emancipation from my mother's path in books, my father had worked to make me into a better-guarded version of the unhappy woman who had birthed me. Meanwhile he had believed for himself and for my brother in what he would refer to as "the glories of science!"—meaning that in planning out the trajectory of my brother's life he had fetishized a certain hard detachment, the compulsive acquisition of dates and facts and a command of numbers, all of which if you asked him were what excused his attitude toward me in the first place, having made it empirically known that girls and women were vulnerable, fragile: that we required rare and often drastic methods of defense. The height of a juniper berry could range from 5.88 to 9.88 millimeters. (My father loved the metric system.) Pluto's mass was a tenth—or wait, perhaps a hundredth—of the earth's. Girl children and the women they threatened to become were feeble creatures designed for locking away and cherishing from a distance while they washed your clothes.

My brother's disappearance hadn't encouraged my father to treat me like a son. When my brother had failed to show up at the property in Middle Village, my father had taken this as additional evidence of our innate divergences in temperament, and as he chewed and swallowed the meat he ordered me to cook for him he made somber speeches about the nobility of what he assumed were my domestic and filial hopes. He knew from the way I cooked that I would be so happy to watch over him in his old age, to mash the root vegetables with a spoon. With care would I test the water of the bath before easing him into it. Did I want to get married? My children would live here; I would already have noted the row house's six bedrooms. The rooms' impossible smallness my father failed to mention; the property had not been chosen for its square footage. I fumed at these epistemological contortions, at my father's presumptive boldness, long before I could name them for what they were.

A mass of clouds was beginning to produce rain, and the dandelions that were still growing in the front yards of the identical homes had started to close to save their petals and pollen from the sort of heavy shower that we hadn't had in almost a month. I hadn't passed by the school on my noon visits to the butcher or the library where my father would ask me to go to return *The Oxford Book of Insects* or *In Quest of Man* or *Houseplants for the Purple Thumb*. The last of these was aimed at me because he considered the work of gardening to be sufficiently feminine. He would sit at night and read to me, choosing long passages that complemented the cloying sentimentality of the book's chapter titles. After "Plants to Nourish and Cherish" came "Where Do Plants Come From?" and I bristled at the writer's diction, which treated the leafy objects like they were babies, suggesting that the presence of a flower or a tree could make up for the absence of another human, and also that nurseries of both types were where a girl like me belonged. I loved my father's plants, but I had come to see that they were not my brothers or sisters any more than the junco I had wished to entice into and keep in a cage. And I had longed to capture and imprison the bird—itself an ambition that in retrospect embarrassed me—because my father was absent and terrific and clueless, not because I was restless with preadolescence and wanted already to become a little mother.

The progress I made in planning was slower because of this way that my brain jumped from one rage-inducing item to the next, but I also held in my mind a constant image of the school, which I had visited not by chance but with purpose in some early evenings since the bird incident. I was familiar with the building's rust-colored brick façade and its few trees lining the walk and with the single air-conditioning unit that filled one of the front windows as well as with the other windows beside it that were simply left open in hot fall weather, as though only the occupants of the teacher's lounge deserved to be cool and comfortable. I pictured throwing open the doors that led inside. With classes in session the hallway would be empty before me: a satisfying void that I could float through like a ghost, the girl no one had known existed.

*

It was simple, the series of actions I intended to take on arriving at the school. I would find the administrative offices, the desks where the principal and the assistant principal and their secretaries sat, and would explain myself with forceful purpose, telling whoever would listen that my father had for his own benefit decided to keep me home; that I was learning nothing except how to prune a front-yard cypress and that even this I had taught myself; that the compact with the board members had been broken and that I wished to enroll immediately in classes, to eat my bologna sandwich with the other children and alongside them to mispronounce the name of the pale, slimy meat I had brought in a paper sack between slices of translucent white bread, pretending I didn't know any better.

All this and more I was prepared to say. It was raining hard, and I had been walking for four blocks but only now was nearing the right turn that would lead to my destination. Ahead I could see the less populated segment of the cemetery grounds whose heart, the section with the weather-stained mausoleums and the older leaning gravestones, sat opposite the school. A few of the mausoleums had half-open doors. They beckoned like little shelters. I had brought no umbrella, and I didn't like the idea of the hem of my skirt dripping when I entered the principal's office, water puddling on the floor as I stood waiting for a stern typist to look up from her gleaming rows of keys. There was a walk signal. Instead of turning right I crossed the street.

The mausoleum I chose was adorned with a name I recognized as belonging to the island where my parents had been born, a space I wanted to but couldn't claim, and it was a name that had something to do with light. The stone structure had fat columns and a doorway framed by what looked like stylized stencil drawings of waves. One of the men whose name hung above the door was a murderer who had died of a heart attack while living in Naples under surveillance by the police, his body transported back across the ocean after being pulled through the streets by a horse. A crowd of hundreds had attended the first of the two funerals, and those who could fit inside the church had stood with their heads bowed in candlelight, the casket covered with thick bunches of flowers that rocked precariously and needed to be strategically positioned and repositioned as the procession made its way to the waiting hearse. The funeral had been filmed and the film released with international distribution, accompanied by sensationalist headlines. In Middle Village, the throng of attendees of the second funeral had swelled to include two thousand men and women and children, people who knew of the man's violence and didn't care or who excused it as necessary, as unavoidable. Someday I would learn all this, but for the moment I only stepped inside and brushed the droplets of water off my clothes. The clouds kept gathering; the rain fell heavy on the roof.

*

I don't know what came over me in the moment when I found myself starting to pluck the flowers from their vases. I had seen them next to Our Lady, Star of the Sea, who stood on a mantle propped up by marble columns that were darker and smaller versions of the ones outside. The engraved letters I touched with my hand had been carved into the stone on both sides of the room, and against the lacquered smoothness of the walls they felt like sandpaper. The engraver's adherence to linguistic norms had intensified when both parents were dead and the siblings had started having to bury each other: *nostra adorata madre, il nostro caro fratello*.

Nostra adorata madre. A beaded rosary hung from the ceiling. I could hear the voice of the neighbor who had been instructed to teach me from a tattered bible while my father was away from home. "Io prendo oggi in testimonio contr'a voi il cielo e la terra," she would recite, playing at godliness, "ch'io ho posta davanti a voi la vita e la morte; la benedizione e la maledizione; eleggete adunque la vita—." *Choose, therefore, life.* That was what she had meant, and I repeated the words in English and they resonated preposterously in the mausoleum as they had in the apartment across the hall from where I used to sleep, the one whose windows had been nailed shut. Was it to prevent me from climbing out onto the fire escape and clambering down to the sidewalk, where I might have been able to run away? I had asked my brother this question and he had mumbled an excuse. Indolent landlords, tenants' rights; it was a song my father also sang. In the mausoleum I was the closest I'd been to the fact of a body's deadness since the day we buried my mother. I remembered this act although I shouldn't have. For a little while my mother's body had been aboveground like these bodies still were, but hers had ended in dirt, in loam that had stunk as my brother held me over it, refusing to call me Beatrice.

"Hello, mamma," I said although she wasn't there.

The ceramic vases on the mantle were full of real blossoms that gleamed in primary colors against the paleness of the stone. One receptacle was white and long-necked; another had been made in the shape of a swan. I reached up and grabbed them both and set them on the floor. I kneeled and with surgical precision removed each individual flower and laid it next to me. New, pretty flowers to the left; sad, wilted, spoiled ones to the right. Soon there was a whole pile of discarded blooms and another pile of fresh roses and lilies and carnations I could choose from as I wove their stems together into a chain. The stems of the newer flowers were crisp like the garden vegetables my father had told me first to nurture and then not to touch. The petals themselves were soft. I ran my fingertips over them. I made the garland long enough that when slipped over my head it would hang down almost to my naval. I alternated between the bright hues and the different species until all at once I was happy, satisfied with what I had made. The feeling was startling and unfamiliar and I smiled and swung open the heavy door.

The mausoleum hadn't yet been outfitted with the stained glass window that the family's surviving members would one day install there, and it was darker inside than it would eventually be, with the result that the beginnings of sunlight that rushed in had what I perceived as a poetic quality and I felt even luckier to be alive. Then I looked down at the necklace of flowers and regretted having forgotten myself.

The roses and lilies and carnations I had chosen had had bright, firm edges and had been untouched by the yellow and brown spots that a girl might find in a bouquet before tossing it in the trash. The blossoms now hanging around my neck were mushy and discolored. They had lost their shape and smelled so rotten that I thought I might throw up.

"What the fuck?" I asked myself out loud. I had learned to swear from my father and had also learned that one of the benefits of spending my days alone was that there was no one to punish me when I copied him.

My father's nighttime reading voice rose from the silence that followed my expletive. A carnation clogged with water could rot, the moisture sticking its petals together, creating a space for the brown spots to thrive and spread. My shirt was soaked with rain; the flowers must have immediately wilted, decomposed. I pretended this made sense. I bent my head and removed the chain of dead blossoms and hung it from a corner of one of the leaning gravestones that people didn't frequent, thinking that with time the petals would dry out and become quaint, an old-fashioned relic, better than nothing.

As I made my way toward the cemetery gate and the noise of the street with the school rising over it in the distance, the worry began to bubble up again. I recognized this sensation; I was characteristically hot. My fingers pulled at each other. I decorated the grass with little pieces of my skin. Unable to stop myself, I bent and yanked a fresh, dry begonia blossom from a potted plant that stood at the foot of one of the newer tree-sheltered monuments. I straightened up and cupped my hands around the begonia and waited.

When I uncurled my fingers again I found that the blossom had transformed itself. The flower was a rotting clump of fibers. The smell was putrid and I dropped the begonia and ran.

*

The problem with popular notions of female hysteria is that they lead both girls and women not to be believed when we discover that our lives have been made a nightmare without our consent. The younger a girl is, the more insistent the objections. She cannot even be imagined not to be lying—not when her own imagination is so vivid, her grasp of reality so tenuous, her sense of the world so warped by a smallness of perspective that the adults have shaken off and are better for having lost. She hears noises in the night; she cultivates invented friends like so many garden plants, and as she grows taller so do the apparitions and no one else can see them. Her mind plays games and is not to be trusted. All this is what the skeptics think, what they think once they are old, even if none of it is true.

Today I am certain that my father spent years poisoning me to make me poisonous, both in the kitchen and in the garden, and that my experience in the cemetery was a result of what he had done. There had been other signs, other events, proofs I had dismissed or forgotten. The look of recognition that the butcher wore when I entered the shop. The boy in the hospital bed—no one could explain what I had done to put him there, but he had bullied my brother, had chased my brother down the street with his jeering friends and then he was lying on the ground and the sirens were rising up around us, getting closer, congesting the air. A dark-eyed junco might nibble at a hemlock seed without dying, but my father had murdered one and sliced it open, the better to understand its insides—how it might then sicken the animal that ate it, or worse. Running from the cemetery I didn't understand all this. I only knew that something was very wrong and that like my father I was somebody who killed things.

I never went back to the cemetery or the school. I still visited the butcher but didn't ask him for bologna for bland sandwiches to tuck into paper bags. Once I had seen him as an ugly enemy as he hung the carcasses from hooks. Now I was in no position to judge him. I avoided touching his hands when taking the packages of meat from him across the counter, unsure of what would happen otherwise. At home I watched over just the plants and trees my father had told me to. In this way I avoided killing any of them, recapturing a kind of equilibrium. Time passed with me alone in the house. I swept and dusted. My father went to work and came home and left again, returning always with traces of gray pigment around the borders of his fingernails, in the same areas where I would chew or pull at my skin, never ceasing to feel nervous.

"How was your day, Bice?" he would ask without looking up as he sliced into the chicken I had baked us or the beef I had pan-fried on the stove. I was eleven now, and he must have known he no longer needed to lace my food with toxins; the process was complete and irreversible.

"Oh, fine," I would say.

"And our plants? The Queen Anne's lace?"

It wasn't Queen Anne's lace, but I pretended to believe him as I pretended to believe everything he said. If I waited too long to answer he would look at me narrowly.

"My lily among the thorns. Don't work too hard, please, figghia mia. You know how delicate you are."

The words my father said were clipped and contradictory; all he asked of me was labor. Still, he raised his head and examined the curves and angles of my face with sudden tenderness, or at least that was what I wanted to see. I didn't care how he treated me, not really, but I wanted to believe that killers could be gentle—that I could be gentle with someone else, in some other time and place. Although my anger at my father was exhausted, I kept hating him and dreaming up ways that I might escape or he might die. After he went to sleep I sat alone at the table or stood as the rain beaded on the one living room window or paced, leafing through a book my father didn't know I could read.

There were millions of girls like me; there was no one else like me.

FIRST NIGHT AT FERN'S SPECTACULAR TWENTY-FOUR-HOUR DINER

Luca Rappa

The local newspaper responded to the opening of the diner with its typical mix of reviews. "Absolutely scrumptious," one food writer proclaimed. "It's a meal," replied another. What more was there to say? The happy guest noted the presence of cheesecake on the menu, the willingness of the waitress to refill his coffee cup without making a corresponding notation on his bill, and the availability of off-street parking. The second reviewer countered that the coffee was lukewarm and accused the fry cook of negligence; his cheeseburger with egg had arrived overdone. I'm sure nothing could have thrilled the editor more than this spirited debate, which accorded with the cosmopolitanism that the paper aspired to, being itself a new addition to the region's roster of dailies and existing uncomfortably as it did in the shadow of the *Times*. I was for my own part just relieved that someone had liked the food, since the woman responsible for the diner's existence had added me to her waitstaff despite my lack of experience and I wasn't eager to look for yet another job.

Platform, road, home: the walk from the station wasn't long, but it took you past cross streets lined with condo buildings whose land-lords had used arson to gentrify them, setting anonymous terrorist blazes that had killed dozens and driven away everyone else. Even if I had been willing to live on one of those streets I wouldn't have been able to afford it, but before departing New York I had saved up a month's rent for a room in a partially abandoned warehouse that once had been a leather factory. Some of its spaces were in disrepair and others were home to creative types or to little businesses whose employees did people's taxes for cheap or spent their days fitting wooden frames around the new paintings of the Manhattanites who were descending on the condo complexes.

My landlord was a sculptor who was living off the proceeds of his dead wife's inheritance. He had rented a block of rooms from the owner of the building with covert plans to renovate and divide and sublet them, envisioning as his tenants the sorts of artists and students who couldn't afford the larger and more professionally finished spaces, and he had hired me to do the labor he couldn't be bothered with. The sculptor was in no hurry—"Take as long as you want," he told me—and so in exchange for rent and a bit of cash I worked my way through the place at a crawl, not wanting the source of my income to end. With deliberate gradualness I raised walls and installed toilets and wired chandeliers and laid carpet and arranged tile in increasingly intricate and time-consuming patterns, trying every moment not to think of my father, who hadn't wanted me to become a contractor but whose opinion mattered less than it would have if I had been speaking to him. The question of my little sister was more problematic; she was helpless and I had gone away without notice, leaving her in the tiny house he'd bought for us in Queens and it depressed me, but I felt the kind of listlessness that you do when something is as inevitable as it is sad, knowing I wouldn't have been of any use to her if I had moved with them from Mulberry Street.

Time blurred and passed: there were no windows in most of the bedrooms and the days had a tendency to run together. Then suddenly one morning there truly was no more work and all the rooms were rented out, my landlord having signed the leases one by one as they were finished, and I was five years older than I'd been.

"I can give you fifteen days to move out," the sculptor said.

"I'll find another job," I told him.

I wanted to stay. The room I'd built for myself was narrow and was windowless like the others, and I slept on a used Hide-a-Bed whose original purchaser had helped me haul it up the three flights of concrete stairs. The bed was convenient because the building wasn't zoned for residential living although my new roommates and I ignored the rules; in the event of an inspection I could tuck away the evidence of where I slept. It was the only place I'd lived on my own.

Somehow I talked my way into a string of retail-adjacent posts in which I stocked shelves with pill bottles and spooned olives into plastic containers. The only catch was that the shops where I began working would close as quickly as their owners hired me. At the now-bankrupt delicatessen, I hung my apron on a nail for the last time as the proprietor's wife and four petite children shook their heads after me, glowering from the back stairway that led to their apartment. He had taken me on against his better judgment. His family was grumbling; I heard the word "curse."

Time blurred and passed some more. The sculptor kept a notebook in his pocket with a tally of the back rent that I owed him.

"I can give you fifteen days to pay," he said.

So I was understandably elated at the diner's grand opening and the glowing review, which the eponymous Fern stapled to a bulletin board with a finality that suggested it was never coming down. I was determined not to let the rebuttal spook me, and I continued scribbling orders and delivering plates to tables and evading the sculptor when I was home.

Evening shifts were more profitable, drawing in legions of inebriated patrons, and were reserved for veteran servers. There wasn't enough work in the late mornings or after the lunch rush on the days I was assigned, which meant that I spent my time moving between the tables and the cash register and the kitchen's triple sink, where I washed the dishes and flatware I had bussed myself because I was the only person on shift besides the cook. Sometimes even the cook himself would disappear; he was temperamental and addicted to nicotine and considered it his right to sit outside the kitchen door on a milk crate in the autumn sun when the thought occurred to him. Then I would crack the eggs into shape in metal rings on the flat top or fish from its receptacle a slimy circle of ground beef, which would look to me like a mess of worms, and lay it sizzling on the grill side.

No one cared, although there was trouble when one day I was made to use the fryolator and in a sequence of mishaps found myself undercooking and serving almost raw a breaded chicken cutlet that from the outside had appeared to be well-done. The offended customer retched into the garbage can beside the register. I imagined unemployment and was desperate enough to consider praying to my estranged family's Catholic god or, if not that, then perhaps to the Blessed Mother, Queen of Heaven, Star of Our Joy. The joy I wanted was the daily meal I was promised—anything off the menu, Fern had said when I was hired, as long as I'd swept and scrubbed the tables and stowed the glossy cuts of meat in the refrigerated cubbies under the prep table.

*

Ask anyone honest and they'll tell you that First Night has been over-taken and in some cases bankrupted by young urban professionals. Intended at its inception to disrupt the tyranny of the champagne glass on December 31st and to provide a venue for urgently good art, First Night had begun in Boston and spread throughout New England and then into the mid-Atlantic states. In its birthplace, before shutting down and being taken over by the local government, it would become a gleaming monstrosity complete with ice sculptures and waterfront fireworks admired by rich partygoers who didn't pay for them. That November in my adopted city, some of the new residents of the condo complexes had conferred and determined that the twenty-four-hour diner, as a venue without a liquor license, was the perfect place for an open mic night and a poetry reading and a count-down to fresh beginnings. It was decided that they'd post flyers on the bulletin board and in similar spots inside the bake shop and the pizzeria, and especially in the restaurant and pub where the town po-ets were rumored most often to congregate on the afternoons when they weren't hidden away in warehouse bedrooms or in the remain-ing tenement apartments. The pub was supposed to be haunted by the ghost of a woman who had died on her wedding day after falling down its flight of stairs, and the young professionals liked to eat and drink there because of this story and because the owner had appren-ticed in Paris, cooking fish at a restaurant where Ernest Hemingway had dined.

"We'll draw them out!" one executive assistant squealed, referring to the poets. Already the residents had established the diner as their planning headquarters, and they were strategizing over chunks of mixed fruit pie.

"We can charge a cover."

This came courtesy of the assistant's boyfriend, another regular, who sat picking the raisins out of each bite of food before he ate it. She punched him in the arm. "Not a cover, Billy. What are you thinking? This is a community event."

She pronounced the word "community" precisely, like it was a precious and delicate object, making fussy gestures with her hands.

"No, what we'll do is—"

I stopped listening. The boyfriend's fork was dangling between his thumb and fingers; he had temporarily given up on eating in hopes of defending his idea, and a clump of fruit and sugar syrup and whipped cream threatened to slide from the four prongs onto the table where it would sit, making the plastic of the table's surface slick and then gummy because he wouldn't bother to wipe up the spill during the two hours the group would remain seated before I could clear their plates. I stared and stared. The boyfriend put down his silverware and I looked away.

The residents went and came and went again, leaving behind a flyer that heralded the arrival of an unforgettable night: BUILD A BETTER NEW YEAR'S! The executive assistant had won this round; entrance was going to be free to anybody who brought with them a song, a poem, or a piece of art.

*

Some days I had other things to do. The division of general studies at the Ivy League university uptown had started offering admission to students who had jobs or had been away from school, and I had written an essay that recounted the story of my leaving home and my employment by the sculptor and the owners of the old-time pharmacy and the delicatessen and the other bankrupted mom-and-pops. The committee must have valued this because they accepted me and made my enrollment financially practical, stressing in the acceptance letter their high standards and their higher hopes for my future.

That fall on my days off I began taking the PATH train to Penn Station and then the Broadway Local to reach the university's brick walkways and black gates. I would fall asleep on the train or the platform holding an open music history textbook or a copy of *The Odyssey*. The courses asserted themselves as a necessary but insufficient condition for happiness while I watched the machinations of the gentrifiers and their landlords. By the third week of December I was nursing the callus I'd developed on my pinkie during an initial semester's worth of essay exams.

The exams also ensured that I was tired throughout a holiday I spent alone. The sophomore girl I had invited over for Christmas Eve had gone home to Long Island instead—"I mean it; call your father," she'd said, like she wasn't nine years younger. I passed the time reading on my bedroom floor next to a potted fir tree the size of a houseplant, which I had decorated with a single sad strand of colored bulbs. After two lonely days I was glad to be exhausted at work, even when my customers, tipsy from the eggnog they'd imbibed before coming in, allowed themselves absurdities that were less covert than usual.

"How did you learn English so well?" one tottering grandmother gushed as I walked her to the register.

I answered her in the standard alternative to my family's language— the one my father understood but refused to speak, and the one our neighbor across the hall had taught us both, my sister and me.

"Sono nato negli Stati Uniti," I said, bowing, a pretended gentleman in a book by Henry James.

She nodded vigorously. "That's wonderful!"

Yes, yes, wonderful. The younger residents of the condo complexes, the ones my age, took longer to return from their time cooking roasts and mulling wine. They were another sort of creature, different from the elderly patrons who came for coffee as early as Boxing Day. But before too long the twenty- and thirty-somethings were swinging open our double doors and we found ourselves squaring off against a new and unspoiled year.

*

The organizers came wearing Baracuta jackets and dresses with shoulder pads that winged out at the edges. The executive assistant's boyfriend sat down with a money tray next to the candy machine that we'd placed at the entrance. One by one the attendees filtered in. Some of them unfolded squares of notebook paper from their pockets; others proffered small canvases which they were instructed to set on a table at the back of the dining room. The canvases were decorated with renderings of mountains and deserts and high plains in fanciful pastel shades; apparently a landscape theme had been suggested. On the makeshift stage we'd erected in one corner, the executive assistant was preparing to sing first: checking her mic, arranging her bangs, testing the high barstool for wobbles. I listened and stopped listening, not wanting to hear the executive assistant attempt Joni's high E.

Instead I circulated like I was supposed to; I took and fulfilled orders. People were letting loose, asking for their cheeseburgers to be topped with an egg despite the warnings of the less enthusiastic reviewer, or else demanding a drizzle of caramel on a dessert that didn't call for it. I was still thinking of my sister, who had never grown any less scrawny even though our father's compulsive desire to feed her had made her tall, and of our father himself, who had tried to make me into a scientist the way he had tried to make my sister dimply and full and protected.

As we approached midnight, some of the pub poets ascended the stage to read from the unfolded squares of paper or from clunkily hand-sewn chapbooks. By that time the orders had been delivered and eaten and the plates swept away, and I was behind the lunch counter leafing through a history book, something assigned for the next semester by the professor who had written it.

Now the executive assistant was at the mic again, giving a tearful speech. The words of the speech wove themselves in with the ones I was reading: "It's been such a lovely evening, and"—*At sixteen, he ran away from home*—"I count myself lucky to live in"—*signs of economic distress and decay*—"this community that so supports its artists."

I continued turning pages. The executive assistant's boyfriend was leaning against the other side of the counter, and he turned his head and bent toward me and hissed.

"Hey, why don't you pay attention? You might learn something."

I didn't respond, but I closed the book. He nodded at me, pleased with himself.

*

There was no one in the parking lot and no one on the street when I left the diner. Inside my employer was pouring non-alcoholic champagne into plastic flutes and distributing them on a tray that she made a show of carrying high above the seated customers' heads. "Here, darlin', take one," she said. "It's beginning to look a lot like New Year's," she said.

She was correct. The executive assistant didn't believe in locking the doors of the car she and the boyfriend shared. A vote of confidence in the neighborhood, I'd heard her call it. I slid into the passenger seat and opened the glove compartment. They'd left the title and their insurance card in an envelope labeled IMPORTANT THINGS, and I took them and their three cassette tapes and the Little Trees air freshener that they'd hung from the rearview mirror and tucked them into the canvas backpack that I brought with me to class.

I walked home although I hadn't been dismissed, heading not to the front entrance but to the old loading dock with its wire garbage cans. I watched as the title and insurance card floated down like feathers. I listened for the plink of each plastic tape against the metal bottom of the can I'd chosen. I lit a match. I knew they could replace the papers and the cassette tapes and the air freshener the next day. It didn't matter. The plastic began to curl and smoke. I thought of the unprosecuted arson: mothers had tossed babies out of windows. I still hadn't been home to my sister. The smoke became a pillar of light and the light became a beacon and I imagined watching it from above. Then I poured a bottle of water over the fire and went back around the side of the building. I let myself in and walked the three flights of stairs to the windowless room, where I remained until it wasn't night.

*

I was on the cutting edge. In a few years the restaurant and pub would also go up in flames, and someone would take a can of spray paint to its boarded-up outer walls. The *Times* quoted the graffiti artist in the Monday paper: "Stox Kaput. Real Estate Next. Bye Bye Yuppies." By then Fern had promoted me to a better schedule; I was mostly through a BA in English and thought of writing under a pseudonym about the night I'd set fire to the couple's belongings. It hadn't been anything but rage, but we needed to burn things down. I was still avoiding Middle Village. A low number of gentrifiers began to flee, scooping up homes in Montclair and Englewood. "We have children," they told each other as they loaded their possessions into boxes. Their tires squealed as they braked and accelerated through the sequence of lights that led them out of the city center, and then like smoke they were gone.

SNAP PEAS

Bice Rappa

Bice was twelve and was standing in the garden, which was where she felt most at home because the garden was small and warm and the bulk of its plants were hers, except that in this moment she didn't feel at home at all because there was blood dripping from her leg onto the unshorn grass, blood like the liquid that had puddled on the kitchen floor on the morning when she was unexpectedly born and she simultaneously knew and didn't know about this, felt that she remembered this sensation although it was strange, and in this moment she and her mother who had died within twenty-four hours of the kitchen episode—she and her mother (let's start again) were identical in all the ways that mattered.

No, this is a lie. Bice was twelve and was standing in the garden, which was where she felt most at home because the garden was small and warm and the bulk of its plants were hers, but in this moment she and her mother were in no way identical. The reasons were several: she was still alive, she was so young that she remained without child or husband, and although her father believed her to be under his control, she had managed to maintain a vivid secret life that he had tried and failed to access, which was why he no longer thought it existed. Bice had been reading books. This was an activity her mother would have enjoyed, would especially have savored in the suppressed language of her own parents. "Nca, Signuri, si riccunta ca cc'era 'na vota 'n Palermu un gran niguzianti maritatu," the mother would have liked to read to her in her bed. "Ora stu gran niguzianti avia 'na figghia, ca comu fu smammata cci vinni 'na sapienza ca ogni cosa chi succidia 'nta la casa, idda avia a dari lu sò disbòtu." *Ever since she had been weaned this daughter had always been able to give a wise opinion about everything that happened in the house.*

Bice's mother and her mother's mother before dying had been too tired for the folktales of Pitrè, but the girl was exhausted in neither the literal nor the figurative sense, and she got up early in the mornings so that she could begin to cook and clean and feed the plants but really so that when her father returned home and she had spent the day with a book or several he could have nothing to say about how she had used her time. She found the books beautiful, even if the borrowed fairy stories she read at first were meant for children half her age and were in simple English rather than in Pitrè's exquisite phrasing. Before the moment in the garden she had already worked her way up on the Lexile scale to a rating of at least 740L. For two years the librarian had been observing the supposedly homeschooled child in the corner at the small table with its red and blue round-seated chairs. There was something magical, she thought, in the ability of this child to teach herself.

After Bice froze in the unshorn grass, she returned to the house and rinsed off her leg and walked with some bounce to this same library—with some bounce because this is a narrative of anger and sometimes self-hatred but not of shame. The paper towel she used to stanch the bleeding was covered with corporate doodles of pineapples and mushrooms and split-open snap peas. In the library she headed for the reference section.

*

At fifteen the girl sat at the dining table with its two leaves tucked into itself, and at this table she was reading about saints. The saints were women and had names like Caterina di Jacopo di Benincasa. They were starving themselves for glory, glory because refusing to eat had not yet begun to be taken as a sign of witchcraft and was instead interpreted as a marker of closeness to god. How gruesome, the way the women were encouraged to vanish by degrees. Bice undressed in front of the house's one mirror and scrutinized her body and despised the thinness it had retained. Lately she had been heaping her plates with too many portions as her father used to, had started mechanically bringing fork to lips when she wasn't hungry. She was chasing substantiality. She wanted to be listened to. "But not at that price," she said in the room where no one else could hear.

Dressed once more, she emerged from the bathroom and went down the stairs, her footsteps thudding on their wooden treads. "I want a tutor," she told her father. He demurred, and the volume of her voice increased. "I want a tutor and I want her yesterday," she said. Someone had died at work and her father had finally been promoted; now some of his days were spent indoors. She threatened to suspend the washing and ironing of his pre-owned pants and shirts. He threatened to expel her from the house. The words were empty and she knew it and the woman arrived the following week, clothed expectedly in black but also carrying her own stack of books.

"Let's begin with some diagnostic exams," the woman suggested. Bice sat across the table, keeping her distance.

*

Imagine: you close your eyes and you are eighteen. Do you see your-self behind the wheel of a car or sipping a drink concocted in a neon hue or maybe lounging in bed with another body, next to which you sigh in the way a phantom would, wondering how you got where you've come to be? Bice was eighteen, but she did and experienced none of these things. She found herself again in the bathroom, this time standing with her arms suspended above her dark head. Her arms made the sort of shape that the arms of a marionette would make; they appeared to be pulled from her elbows by a string that was too thin to see. With her left hand she was holding a strand of white hair, which she pinched between a thumb and two fingertips. In her right hand she held a tweezer: it was bubblegum pink and was emblazoned at one end with the word CARE. Over and over she bent toward the image of herself in the one mirror, then located a hair and yanked. The white strands disordered the tile floor, which resembled the floor where her mother would faint when pregnant. But Bice was not pregnant, hadn't so much as glanced at a possible lover because she was afraid of what would happen, not just to her but to them.

The hairs sprouted with alarming frequency, and their appearance was followed without fail by a flash of metal in the bathroom light. There was a time when Bice's left eye had been assertively rather than slightly blue-brown. Then she had been a marvel recently manifest-ed; then she had been the surviving infant. Now the difference in her irises was subtle, could be seen only at close distance—which sounds like a contradiction in terms, but think of the phrase as it's used in photography and film and you'll begin to grasp how she viewed her-self, as the subject of a surreal visual text. How unnatural, the speed at which the new hairs regenerated and the old ones lost their pigment.

Soon she noticed that the diameter of her ponytail was shrinking. She discovered that she needed to leave the hairs alone unless she wanted to become bald in patches, which would be worse. The glints of blue and white shone undeterred.

*

She reached twenty-one, which for her meant graduating from the Grimms to the stories her mother would so have loved, to "Caterina la sapienti" and "La panza chi parra" and "Peppi, spersu pri lu munnu." *Peppi, lost in the world.* Lost in the world is what the girl wished that she were. She had made the tutor teach her the vanishing language alongside the two the tutor claimed were useful. Another story featured a succession of vegetables that by magic turned men and women either into donkeys or back into the people they used to be. Bice still felt most at home in the garden, and she loved the stories because they were as strange as she was. She didn't love her father, who had had the audacity to trap her in the house and its two yards, or her mother, who had had the audacity to die.

*

For two months Bice had been twenty-four. She had taken up singing, and her idea of rebellion was to sit in a darkened theater in the middle of the day, with strangers all around her although this felt dangerous, and she and the strangers were watching as a woman who was not yet forty pretended to be an old witch. "I'm going," she had told her father, holding the cashbox. The witch was obsessed with vegetables, with rampion and rutabaga. The woman's face was breathless red; Bice held her own breath in. At intermission she paced up and down the sidewalk. She took in the spectacle of a giant boot, the cabs rushing one way, the too-warm air.

The girl went back into the dark, where the sound split her open when it ended, its audience clapping wildly, and then she disappeared underground and resurfaced on Metropolitan Avenue. There she walked until she regained not the row house but the garden she glided through the house to reach. The corner she avoided was the one with the edible plants. That corner of the garden was a danger scene.

*

All that year she wrote to an audience of herself. *Dear B—, I am waiting for something to happen*. In February a supernova had appeared that casual observers could see from the decks and chimineas of their backyards. Soon there would be five billion babies and young people and old people on the planet. This later would turn out to be unimpressive. September: her birthday, and in a cluster of buildings surrounded by desert peaks, stakeholders had gathered to discuss the possibilities of artificial life. The garden hose had spun hot and wrestled itself out of her hands. The pope had arrived in Los Angeles, blinking amid the palms; he'd waved from a truck bed encased in glass. A woman had swum for hours through the Bering Strait. She had envisioned the act as a political gesture, her arms and legs cutting the water away from her body.

After her matinee Bice tapped and tapped her pencil; she was a thief at her father's desk. She sang over the fence at the neighbors who had never liked her, who glanced at each other when she lay in the dirt. There was an old bicycle in the cellar and she considered hoisting it to her shoulder, considered carrying it that way up the stairs and through the bulkhead to the street where if she was lucky she might ride even if no one had bothered to teach her. Then it was no longer 1987. She kept on waiting for something to occur. She wrote, *I want a lover to slap in the face*. The pope was talking about abstinence.

Somewhere the swimmer was eating oatmeal that was thick with apples. *Maybe I'll burn all the meats on the stove.* She was learning to be theatrical; she was all inconstancies. She was waiting for her number to come up.

PART 2: 1989-1991

LUNCH BUCKET

Gina Puglisi

"You look like death; go the fuck home." We were a Greek chorus chanting, forming a ring around the newly anointed manager. "You'll get us all sick. We'll hate you. Trust us."

If he hurried he could make it before the rain started for fucking real. This was what we said as we leaned over tables and chairs and peered out the diner's front windows. Speaking this way was not a job-threatening move because the manager had been one of us until a week ago and he was picky about some things but was not the sort of person to get precious about an obscenity. Some of us had been to the former factory where the manager lived; parties among the staff at Fern's weren't unheard of on a Tuesday night when the list of needed servers and dishwashers and fry cooks was short. We knew him well enough to know that he would love us for mobilizing en masse to take him by the shoulders, for walking him backward out from behind the counter and between the exactingly arranged rows of seating until, still facing us and still facing away from the two doors, he found his body thrust through them and dumped onto the sidewalk. "Do not pass 'go'—do not collect \$200," we told him. "Just go the fuck home."

We had had a feeling that this was going to be a good year although it was a year like a bad birthday, one of those birthdays that celebrate an insignificant age and that float by without anything substantial happening. Search the internet for mentions of our city of residence together with this particular year, and the first half-dozen results will refer to a single concert that Nirvana played at a bar that had been a tavern for factory workers but that soon would be declared the "Best Club in New York—Even Though It's in New Jersey." The band posed in front of the water and the other, more impressive city, with its frontman positioned in the back so that he looked smaller-boned than his fellow musicians. Cars parked on both sides of the slanted cobblestone streets that the Manhattan girls didn't like to walk in heels. The cars had narrow bumpers and now look used in pictures even when they weren't at the time the pictures were taken. Some of us had been here for twenty or thirty years and had lived through childhoods dotted with trips to restaurants similar to the business that now employed us. Our mothers had carted us there along with the friends' children they were watching for extra cash. Our fathers had brought us in for meals instead of cooking, so that we were sitting at these tables and not at home when we learned to dip chicken in honey or make a seal over the top of a straw with our pinkies. Other servers were newer transplants and were more likely to be found scribbling a poem in free verse on the back of a napkin in the walk-in fridge.

Everyone was satisfied with the newly anointed manager, whom we also suspected of being a writer but who had been at Fern's so long that he deserved to be in charge of devising schedules and editing menus and fielding complaints about the temperature of the food. We spent the first three days of his absence joking about how angry he would be to learn what he'd missed out on in tips. The conversation shifted in tone when it got to be the end of the week and he hadn't yet come back to us. Fern's Friday night slots were the most coveted; they were when we earned our best income from the drunken demi-heiresses and their fiancés, who liked to imagine themselves as living dangerously if they left their condominiums for a midnight snack. We drew straws and before I knew it I was being asked to walk through twenty-nine minutes of darkness from the diner to the warehouse building where our disappeared leader was expected to be.

"Really, friends, do we think this is necessary?"

I wasn't pleased with the role they'd assigned me or the impending cold or the absence of light outside.

"Gina, he's missing a Friday. The condo clientele are back."

"They have their wallets out. The girls spent the afternoon hot-rollering their hair."

"Something is very wrong, Gina. Are we going to let this stand?"

No, of course not. I took my beat-up excuse for a purse and slung it over my shoulder and left.

*

They all assumed that their manager was actually fine. None of them could have guessed what Gina would discover in the neglected factory. Not wanting to seem callous, I'd prefer to believe each of these statements: that my coworkers' concern was actually playful, manufactured out of a desire for fun. Any of us would have been surprised to walk up too many flights of unfinished stairs and find our neat and presentable leader with his head in a trash can that he carried with him as he opened the door, vomiting.

"Hey, kiddo," he managed to raise his head to say.

Every response I could come up with was obvious and unhelpful.

"Jesus, dude, you look like shit."

That was what I settled on as I helped him back through the badly carpeted hallway, past the stairs and into the room where he slept. I stepped in and knew right away that they had laid the carpet themselves and hadn't had it cleaned since. The room wasn't built to be stayed in; its lack of windows made it claustrophobic. "When's the last time you got out?" I posed the question as though I couldn't infer the answer. We had ejected him from the diner four days before; for four days he had been throwing up and attempting broth and crackers and throwing up again.

It was good that I didn't expect a reply, since I would have had to wait for him to double over from his worn spot on the couch and heave once more into the can and straighten back up to look at me. As things stood I sat not waiting while our manager produced tortured sounds that made me ask myself if he was going to die. His facial skin was dry and red and was peeling where he had scratched it. His forehead was sweatless. There had been nights when I'd woken up at 3 a.m. after a too-raw burger at Corner Bistro. I knew what that looked like. This was not that.

"Are you keeping down fluids?"

I should say at this point that I am not a mystical healer of men. In the kitchen, which was also bizarrely carpeted and where I poured a glass of water from the tap, I noted the dirty metal cutlery in the larger garbage can. Someone was throwing away forks and spoons with the remains of microwaveable meals because they couldn't be bothered to clean them. I resolved not to do any dishes while I was there.

Reopening the door to the room, I saw the newly anointed manager lying prone on the wood floor. "Okay, champ," I said, selecting the word because it was the sort of sympathetic term a man might use with another man without promising him any prolonged care or affection. "Maybe let's go to the hospital."

He moaned something about insurance, which none of us had.

"Don't be cheap. You're missing Friday night for this." Another moan. "Come on. Just—get—up."

Now I was kicking the back of his thigh with the toe of my right sneaker. He didn't say anything more, only flinched a little, and I realized he was falling asleep. "Jesus," I repeated.

For a while I sat cross-legged beside him, keeping watch, making sure he was breathing in and out. I scratched my fingernails against the carpet; I drank from the glass of water that he hadn't touched. I'll confess that I left him alone when I went to find a bathroom and wandered up the rickety internal stairway to the second floor and its one operational toilet. The large open space at the top of the stairs was taken up by a trampoline in a size I hadn't known they made. The walls were decorated with half-painted canvases done in a pop-art style that was derivative not of Warhol or Lichtenstein but of somebody I couldn't place. The bathroom was at the end of a long hall, and inside I spent too long staring at myself in the frameless mirror and feeling drunk although I wasn't.

When I came back down the newly anointed manager was gone. He wasn't sitting on the worn-out couch or lying collapsed on the bedroom floor or the kitchen carpet. I walked the hallways calling his name. It was still dark outside the tall factory windows, but the inside lights were on and blazing.

"Hello? Anybody?"

All of a sudden my legs were too tired to support me and I sank and folded my body into a compact package outside the manager's metal bedroom door. I brought my knees to my chest and tucked my chin like I was about to cannonball into the water between our city and the real one. I sat there like I'd sat next to the manager, thinking about what kind of sucker would stick around.

As far as I could tell, there was no one home.

*

The chorus was in fine form on Sunday when our missing leader emerged and rejoined the ranks of the living and serving. We had started to bicker about the shift schedule's logic and the feasibility of adding Swedish pancakes to the menu of a restaurant that with time was becoming more popular with customers our age than it was with retired Scandinavians. On some days they seemed like us, the younger customers, and we shook our heads and muttered. "No more pancakes," we said. Then we would remember that these were people whose passion for croquet was being written about in newspapers and we'd be plunged again into uncertainty; who knew what they actually wanted? "Thank god," someone declared when the manager strode in. I was the only one who was pissed, who had waited for five hours between sleep and boredom before assuming that the manager was dead on a street corner and allowing myself to stumble back to the apartment where I was renting a room.

I hissed at him over a trough of dirty lettuce in the back of the kitchen.

"Dude, where the hell did you go?"

There was one cook on, and as usual the cook preferred to smoke rather than wash his own vegetables. "Can't one of the girls do it?" he had asked no one in particular, but I'd volunteered the manager and grabbed him by the sleeve and forced him with me through the bump door that led out of the diners' view.

"Oh, Gina. What are you talking about?"

The manager kept sighing. I sputtered and swore but couldn't get him to admit that he had left the eyesore of a warehouse while I was in the bathroom or even to admit that I had been there. No one else had seen me either, he said. No one had so much as mentioned a girl of my description. He had roommates; he had a landlord who was inconveniently omnipresent. Was I sure this hadn't been a dream? I was a compassionate person; perhaps worry had invaded my subconscious. Asked to vouch for me, my colleagues could only say that I had exited in a huff after drawing the short straw.

Every shift became an opportunity for me to chase the validation I craved. I described to the manager the unfinished concrete of the external stairs and the precariousness of the interior ones. I described and critiqued the roommates' forays into painting. I pointed out my intimate knowledge of the trampoline and its size. He granted that I must at some point have visited him at home, but he also had an answer for this.

"Didn't you come to one of our house parties last summer?"

I hadn't.

*

Eventually I found new employment. The library in my aunt's part of Queens had lost a staff member so unexpectedly that they overlooked my lack of qualifications outside of food service, and I threw out most of what I owned and packed the rest into two boxes that I tossed in the trunk of a cab paid for with the end of my tips.

Everyone's stories were ending with moves to and from and across the other city, the real city, and I didn't want to be everyone but also couldn't stand the manager's mild-mannered condescension. On my way out of the dining room on my last day, I lingered behind a customer at the register while the manager rang her up. She took her change and flounced down the aisle between the clusters of eating guests; her food had taken longer than she'd wanted. I waited for the door to close behind her and for him to speak.

"No hard feelings, Gina. You're a sweet girl."

I would like to be able to say that I stabbed him. *I rammed a kitchen knife deep into the cavity of his chest*. In reality I only looked at him like he had looked at me raising his head out of the plastic bin. As if I was going to be sick. I gave him a look that was like vomiting and I turned and walked out channeling the woman customer, bumping against chairs and tables not to signal that I was angry but to show that I still existed: how well I could take up space.

ELECTRIC DRIP

Bice Rappa

They were quite a pair: the new-new girl and the one whose breathing killed the plants. Bice remembered what it had been like when she'd first arrived in Middle Village. Average was how she had thought of the row houses and the stunted trees on their chosen block, her excitement at being allowed outdoors giving way to rapid disenchantment. The new-new girl was different; apparently she took the area's normalcy in stride. She was living with a sister of her father's who hadn't had a child and who was gloriously unconcerned with when she arrived at and departed the house and where she was headed once she left, with what she ate and drank and its consequences for her figure, with how much money she made and whether she could pay the rent that she hadn't been asked to contribute. So it hadn't been a systemic shock, this experience of relinquishing her room in an apartment in a neighboring state to move in with someone born during the year when Sno Balls were invented. And besides, in going there to live the new-new girl had been able to leave a job she hated, which had made her displacement almost thrilling instead of sad.

The move had become achievable when, during a very competitive game of Trivial Pursuit, the new-new girl's maiden aunt had coaxed and then bribed a librarian friend into making the girl her assistant. "I'll throw the game," she'd whispered into the librarian's ear as they stood in the kitchen during a pause in play. The librarian had replied without an iota of hesitation; the deal was done, and Gina in an instant became the sort of person who wore pencil skirts to work instead of a uniform with stripes.

It was basically preordained that Bice and the new-new girl would meet. Bice had loved reading borrowed books for sixteen years, although she now haunted the section of the library devoted to foreign languages and not the primary-hued side. The designers of children's wings of American library buildings had been busy creating spaces known for bright, carpeted stairs that led to nooks with short shelves and giant sacks filled with rattling fake beans. The spot where Bice installed herself was carpeted and tiled in shades of putty and had tables whose chairs would hurt the middle region of your spine if you sat there too long. She would leave kneading her back with her fist or otherwise would have to get up and pace with a volume she wanted to read but didn't want to bring home, which was how she noticed Gina, whose face she hadn't seen before and who was staring at her from behind the checkout counter without attempting to hide it.

"Try not to wear a hole in the carpet," Gina said. She was experimenting with the acerbic delivery that in childhood they both had thought was the province of all library staff.

Bice examined the teenage-looking features and the muted cardigan above which they incongruously floated. She rolled her eyes.

"Did you borrow that sweater from your mother?"

As someone whose better parent was long dead, Bice knew how to lace the word "mother" with a special kind of malice if provoked. The new-new girl had been flipping through a sheaf of typewritten catalog cards, and her hands lingered on one of them and she looked up with a helplessness that made Bice sorry.

"From my aunt," said the librarian's assistant.

"Let's get coffee," suggested Bice.

Gina never told strangers the true story of what she had been doing when her mother and her father disappeared. In some versions she had been lying on a window seat in the bedroom of a wealthier friend, bouncing her foot up and down to the rhythm of the friend's chatter about a love interest—rather than the details, what mattered was that she had been innocent, listening, performing a sympathetic act. At other times she fabricated wilder narratives that involved extreme sports or additional tragedies: she had been bungee jumping, cliff diving, burying the body of a beloved horse. She didn't say that she had fought with her mother and her father about some forgettable topic and, being an adolescent, had taken their one car without permission, driving it for two hours before crashing into a tree outside the entrance to Emmell's Septic Landfill. She didn't say that her mother and her father had set out searching for her on foot because she hadn't returned and night was falling and they were at bottom decent people who had wrongly intuited that she was stranded somewhere nearby; that the note she would later discover in her mother's handwriting on the kitchen counter in their rented three-bedroom was the sole evidence of where they had gone and for what reason; or that half a decade on, their whereabouts continued to be as mysterious as their vanishing was her fault. The new-new girl didn't say any of this yet to Bice as she leaned back and watched her spill the hot beverage from her spoon onto the ceramic top of the outdoor table she had insisted they request.

"I used to work at a place like this," Gina told her. (Here was the truth.) "My parents were the owners, but that was before they were attacked by a rabid dog." (Two blatant lies.) Bice nodded, playing along. It was the first time she'd had coffee or tea with someone other than her father.

*

The challenges started as a form of entertainment. The new-new girl turned twenty-three and, walking sleepy into her aunt's empty living room, found an envelope marked with her name propped up on the coffee table against the spine of a hardcover book about the Beach Boys. The envelope contained the months' worth of rent she had insisted on trying to pay, which her aunt now insisted on returning as a present, and instead of arguing she took the bus to the used car dealership where she had seen a Volvo so rusted, so hideous that she could purchase it with half of what she had. Parallel parked outside the Sherwin-Williams on a Sunday, she and Bice attacked the sides of the car with sandpaper and then with primer and with paint the color of a fantastical twilight. Bice claimed the driver's side, yelling commands like "Stay in your area!" and "Watch out!" and "I've got this part!" until Gina finally lost it.

"Okay, dude, what's your problem?" she half-shouted from behind the left rear wheel. "Seriously, spill."

Bice paused, sprayed, paused.

"So, here's the thing—"

Gina acted more intrigued than dissuaded by Bice's stories of the neighborhood boys and flowers she'd touched or merely breathed on that had then collapsed or vomited or wilted. Within a day she showed up again at the house on 67th Road, this time in rumpled work clothes. The backseat of the sedan was piled with bunches of still-fresh blossoms dug out of a dumpster behind Met Foods.

"Let's test this out," she suggested, proffering a red carnation from the stoop. She watched as Bice inhaled and exhaled and the straight stem of the flower became a hook finished off with a clump of ragged petals. "Bedda matri—you're not wrong," said the new-new girl, whose parents and their siblings had been late arrivals from the same island that had chewed up the Rappas and spat them out. She and Bice repeated the experiment with a lily and a yellow rose whose corolla turned a dusky crinkled orange around the edges before Bice's third breath.

The fun part, once they knew they weren't imagining things, was testing the impact of the trick on each other. Bice held a hand up to her mouth and exhaled. Nothing. Gina held a hand to Bice's lips and saw a red blotch bloom. They were standing six inches apart on the tiny lawn, facing each other and pretending to talk about the weather, when Gina reported becoming woozy and nauseous. She pushed Bice away in time: exclaiming, delighted.

At a distance of a foot they could chat for three minutes like their mothers would have in the yard before Gina began feeling ill. From two feet away Bice could carry on an entire conversation without seeming to poison anyone. It was the same if they stood side by side instead of face to face. This made sense, Bice said. She had gone to West 45th Street to see a play; no one next to her had keeled over in their chair.

They experimented with touch. Although Bice could hold a flower by its tough, protective stem, she couldn't touch its petals even if she didn't blow on them. And she couldn't follow the trail of a wrinkle in the new-new girl's palm without triggering a hive or a pimple or a bruise. But the power was just in her hands. They could lean against each other normally, even bare-skinned, giggling like members of a cheer squad.

"Breathe on me," Gina would say when she started getting bored.

She seemed to enjoy the feeling, anticipating the split second when the scene would fade to almost black and she'd have to choose whether to recapture herself. They avoided the question of how Bice had gotten this way like Gina still avoided the question of her parents.

Bice didn't have a license, but they took turns driving above the speed limit to hear the car's motor whinge. Whoever's turn it was would keep the windows down and the heat on because it was just April but they wanted to feel the air rush through the cabin. Bice would swivel her head and Gina would laugh again, punching her upper arm because she could. "Don't look at me, creature," Gina always squealed. It was obvious that she liked pressing her tongue against the roof of her mouth as she pronounced the word. Once it rained when they had planned a day trip to Atlantic Beach and they went anyway, conscious of and indifferent to how predictable they were. Water dripped from the window frames onto the doors' blue upholstery. Bice stretched her arm out and let the wind pull her hand back until it hurt. She had been watching Gina and had become determined to discover what it felt like, being kind and fragile and cruel and reckless all at once. The younger driver treated her like they were just the same: two deadly girls.

*

The work hours of Bice's mason father prevented him from knowing where his daughter went. The new-new girl made the best of his schedule, cajoling the real librarian into giving her evening shifts so that during the day Bice and Gina could drive the car to upstate flea markets or the Astoria pool, with its outdoor view of the bridge that hadn't yet been renamed for an assassinated senator. Having nowhere in mind they drove over the bridge, past the psychiatric center that once had been a hospital for immigrants and past the pollution control plant and the remains of Little Hell Gate, before doubling back and returning to the place where they'd started. The bridge's suspender cables stretched up to dizzy heights and then receded as the towers of the former hospital came into view.

Gina would honk and shift and swear she could walk the bridge from end to end balanced on the main cable. Bice would catch herself picturing what would happen if her father came down with a fever or injured a hand or was fired or for some other reason arrived home early to find her gone, and the idea of his anger was arresting and she would stop whatever they were doing and say, "Take me back, please, Gina; oh god." In the middle of a daytime showing of a science fiction western featuring a cast of variously lovelorn and visionary time travelers, Bice felt her throat constrict. A cold sweat stuck her shirt to the ridges of her shoulder blades. She tried to remember what it was supposed to feel like to inhale, was convinced that if she stopped thinking *in—out—in* her lungs would quit, that for her the mechanism of breath was no longer autonomic. She fled the building. As a steam locomotive propelled the famed vehicle and its gull-wing doors into another century, she stood outside with her back against the brick wall of the theater's facade.

"It's normal," Gina had yelled as she trailed behind her.

"Don't you get it?" Now they were standing there together, and Bice grabbed her by her bare shoulders and shook. "None of this is normal!"

Red bumps emerged in the spots where Bice's fingers had been. The new-new girl turned her head and tilted her chin and stared down at the sudden pustules.

"Great. Absolutely terrific."

Not looking back, she crossed the sidewalk and the road they'd parallel parked on. Bice followed her, moving slowly as she breathed.

"I'm sorry," she called. Then louder: "I said I'm sorry!"

*

Gina sat in the hot car until Bice reappeared at the passenger-side window. *I'm sorry*, she mouthed again. She opened the door and climbed in. The velour of the bucket seat was crusted, and she picked at it and at the skin around her nails.

Gina didn't move. The rash was weeping.

"I think I killed my parents," Gina told her.

"I know," said Bice.

"It's crazy how people leave you."

"I know. I know."

The new-new girl was quiet. She started the car and shifted into reverse and backed up and turned the wheel. They didn't speak during the time it took to return Bice to the front steps of her father's house. They went down Metropolitan Avenue gazing out at the blocks of squat buildings whose brickwork her father could have done.

There was the cemetery. Yes, really; this is what you drive through when you take the main street home to 67th Road from the Cinemart in Forest Hills. You can't avoid it. The crypts and gravestones shine from their fenced-in places on either side of the street, and you may have gone to the movies to take in a romantic comedy or an action flick about an aging New York cop, but when you return to Middle Village this is what you see. Bice and Gina were no different and they drove slowly by and continued saying nothing. There was no room to park where the house and its siding rose up over the yard, and Bice slid out of the car like she had slid into it, without noise or sound.

DONUT

Gina Puglisi

Gina played the crash like a video game. Say it again, with the cadence of a chant at recess: "Gina played the crash like a vid-e-o game." The road to the south of the state was straight and boring and extended through a wasteland of white and billowing smokestacks. In childhood she had been placed in her parents' only car for trips that should have involved air travel but that for them required hours on the highway, and the hours would stretch on in stopped traffic unless they departed late. The sky would be black like pitch and she would fall asleep mouthing *Breathe, breathe in the air* and wake up an hour later in the middle of industrial hell, Clare Tory singing without words. Driving mad on her own she took the curves of the junctions between the turnpike and the other fast roads like progressively speedier levels in a virtual racecourse. The series of lanes wasn't a rainbow but the space beyond them was just as empty. The stars made the nothing night criminal. She was off the last highway now and was on a narrow road that was often still straight but was filled with dangers. She spun out; she came to; she felt something wrong. Against all wisdom she drove the wreck home. There was no one inside of the rented duplex.

At the station they offered her a Long John; for a moment she was one of them. Then she was a sad orphan, a lost one. She was taking the curves of the junctions between the expressway and the other roads, driving forward and then backward in her head. Holding the B button, gliding like she was on rails, into a rewinding dark.

SUGARPLUM

Luca Rappa

When the nightmares started was when I realized I was in trouble. For months I had been employing sleep as a pillowy refuge from my obsessive thoughts and the self-loathing they inspired. I would lay my head down and wander through a mundane dreamworld populated with acceptable versions of my life: versions in which I adopted a kitten and drove my father to the office of his urologist and cooked elaborate vegetarian meals. In another string of dreams I was a girl, a girl with obligatory and sequential aspirations, like the goal of being cast as Clara in *The Nutcracker* and invited on a dinner date. Sometimes I sleepwalked during dreams and woke up chastised or rescued from whatever chance of death by a roommate or a neighbor. At no time before waking did I become cognizant of the possibility that the dreams might be odd, that the universe of events or the personality my brain was inventing might be unreal. I dreamed and dreamed and in dreams did not think of the worst that could happen or of myself as broken for doing so. When I did wake I often found that I felt renewed and ready, or as ready as I could be, to encounter the corners of my uglier conscious mind. *That's interesting*, I would reply without speaking, addressing myself as the intake therapist had suggested during my first and final appointment.

Then a mirror in my house fell and broke into a thousand shards. I don't mean this in a metaphorical sense; I had hung the mirror on a screw in the hallway of the converted factory apartment where I was still living with a dozen other tenants, and the mirror remained in place through all the slammed doors rattling the wall I'd raised despite not being licensed as a contractor, until one night during an explosive argument between the apartment's two youngest residents—who everybody knew were sleeping together although none of us expected them to admit it—the mirror shuddered and wobbled and came down. The tiny shards and large, jagged slabs of glass bounced off the tiles I'd laid and the grout between them, and the two youngest residents screamed. The rest of us ran into the hallway in various states of semi-dress. The second-youngest resident's foot was bleeding.

"Fucking fuck," said the owner of the foot. The youngest resident was visibly chastened, having started the argument in the first place. I swept up the smaller fragments. They were fine, powdery. Sleeping on the Hide-a-Bed that night I dreamed of ground glass poisoning a child's food. In the dream I couldn't recall that this was a myth, something debunked by expert murderers themselves in the city across the Hudson.

The following sleep I dreamed of the same girl's face and neck coated in red; the shards and slabs had rained from an unfathomable ceiling. On the third night we were all swimming in glass—in our waking lives, the trampoline on the second floor of our residence had been replaced with an aboveground swimming pool for a house party—and the other residents and I and the child whom I wasn't acquainted with even in the dream but who was still mysteriously there, all of us had bodies that were blood-laden although we swam and smiled as if nothing were wrong in any way. I kept waking up with a gasp, unable to swallow. My mouth full of ground mirror.

*

Because I didn't know what to do without the safety of my happier unconscious flights, I took up running on the days and in the early and late evenings when I wasn't expected to show up at the diner where I'd been made the manager. I ran on sidewalks and sometimes in the street past shuttered businesses with little green awnings and row houses sided with stone or vinyl and flowerpots out of which plants that were dry and decaying most often spilled. It was fall but warm, and the state of the flowers seemed a likely sign of neglect; after seeing them I ran faster and my running faster was problematic because I was out of shape and would often end a run with my head between my knees.

The first IPCC report had come out in August and was grave in its expressions of concern about greenhouse gases and global mean temperature as well as in its uncertainty about the impacts of the chemical compounds on polar ice sheets and oceans and clouds. I had photocopied all 365 pages of the report at the library on the corner of Park and 5th Street, which bordered a wooded square that looked as though it belonged in New England. The copy of the report was lying in my room on top of the board balanced on two cinderblocks that I used for writing, and it was another reason why I wouldn't go home and why my feet moved themselves more quickly when I saw the wilted plants, which by mid-October were also soggy from three inches of rain. I ran and stopped and huffed and ran again, trying to clear my head of environmental disaster, of my own abnormality, of girls with glass in their hair. I murmured hello to elderly women on the corner.

You'll notice that I haven't been specific about the worst of the thoughts that followed me around. This obfuscation stems partly from a stubborn-rooted shame and partly from the words of the intake therapist, who before I fled his office assured me that confessing the most terrifying contents of my brain was a shortcut to psychological hell. My desire to disclose these items, he explained, was more than a remnant of my family's halfhearted and my own lapsed Catholicism. "You want someone to reassure you that you're normal," he commented as he ripped the handwritten prescription for fluvoxamine from the pad of white sheets. The impulse to let myself be judged would never ease if I yielded to it, he said. I would only make it worse, he said. The intake therapist lowered his spectacles and looked at me with cinematic sternness, no doubt conscious of having by far transgressed the usual boundaries of a diagnostic session. I was glad I'd worn my running shoes to the office because I didn't believe him about the dangers of disclosure and I felt a sudden urge to sprint away. But the repeated worsening of my condition isn't something I can risk, so on the off chance that the man is right—well, you understand. What I can tell you is that I began storing up the exhaustion I would experience after a run, the numb sense of detachment and relief. Alone in my bed I would call up and attempt to drown in the feeling, imagining myself outside the sad sack of my body. Then I would try to conjure better dreams again, to will them into existence the way the crash-bang of the mirror had planted nightmares in me.

*

After a long time they worked, the madcap brain escapes. Of all the places I forced my unconscious to go while I was sleeping, the one I most appreciated was the void of outer space. In this recurrent episode I would take the A/C/E to West 4th Street and the F train to Delancey and the M train to its terminal stop, where after much walking I would find my estranged kid sister deep in Queens. She would be sitting on the stoop eating grapes like our dead mother used to do.

"Hello, Sugarplum," I would inexplicably say. "Let's get the hell out of here."

She would understand what I meant and realize that I meant it and would only nod, agreeing, following me back on the sequence of trains and then to the mission launchpad that of course would be located in the middle bedroom of a railroad apartment on the Upper West Side. "You're so good at this," she would say as we suited up, and I would know that "this" was brothering. As we watched the baking earth recede out the rear window, she would cover my hand with hers and gaze up at me and smile.

"We did it," she would tell me.

"Together," I'd say.

By morning my sister would be gone. December 23rd, and it was 66 degrees across the Hudson. I continued to run and dream and started hoping that the next dream would be the one that didn't end. It would zigzag before me like a rocket trail, refracting light from the mesosphere after sunset. Exploded and exquisite, when it was already night on earth.

LA SIGNURINA NUN AVI FAMI

Bice Rappa

Bice was at the table again, and she was sitting and reading a novel. The novel she was reading was about a Genevan university student with scientific ambitions and an excess of unprocessed grief. Bice was reading in fits and starts as again and again her father asked questions that by design prompted her to look up from the book whose spine she had already broken. She would feel a disorienting mix of hope and annoyance at the sound of her father's voice; her father was not often engaging and engagement was what she wanted, being lonely, but on the other hand she was occupied with the story and was nervously anticipating what she felt certain would be the Genevan university student's maladaptive methods of recovery. Now the university student was a full-fledged scientist and was conducting dangerous experiments without knowing that this would kill him, would kill him because—well, because playing god is inadvisable and can have unanticipated results. The result the full-fledged scientist attained was enough to engender self-hatred. It made him flee the town. Bice read on, and as she read she envisioned her own face as the face of the creature. There was something unsettling about the ways the girl and the creature resembled each other, like they might at any time turn out to be twins. For her this would be a disaster. The creature wasn't a year old and was already too far gone. Bice flipped pages she'd skimmed instead of reading. "Ai fami?" her father asked her. He always asked her; he also answered himself. Always the answer stayed the same.

CENTER CUT

Quinn O'Leary

In Middle Village it was still summer, but it was a Sunday and on Sundays she didn't come into the shop, and because he wouldn't see the girl during either the morning or the afternoon or just at the midpoint of the day the butcher felt deflated as the hours crawled by, which is to say that he was uninterested in reading or in filling in the blank squares of a crossword or in calling his mother on the telephone that his father had mounted in the left corner behind the marbled and bloody meats. The shop had belonged to Quinn's father and there had never been any question about whether he would take it over even though doing this would have obvious consequences, such as the fear he would inspire in children and the difficulty he would have finding a girlfriend.

These days the girl and he were almost of an age. When her family had moved to town he had just turned seventeen although he had been working after school and then full-time in the shop since he was twelve. Now seventeen more years had passed, and the girl was just shy of twenty-seven and the butcher wasn't thirty-five. His father's brother had died after reaching what was now the American age of majority, and this meant that every year Quinn survived was a year his father breathed a sigh of relief. The family tragedy had been one of the not-so-subtle reasons why his father had demanded that Quinn replace him in the shop rather than letting him go to a school of art and design, although without his red-stained apron and hands the butcher was a punk. Donning the uniform each morning he sensed himself getting metaphysically older and older until he was pinching the cheeks of toddlers and winking in a way that suggested that his customers had traveled back in time to a moment when there might be a drugstore with a soda fountain down the block. When he could get away from the shop he wore Doc Martens and a leather jacket and distressed tee-shirts and jeans with ripped knees. He still lived above the shop unlike his mother and his father, who had had the decency to move out of the apartment and into a house with a modest footprint. At twenty-six he had floated the idea of a mohawk and had been rejected: "Who will buy poultry from an anarchist?" his father had asked. His mother had sniffed and frowned, insinuating that she was about to cry.

*

Quinn chose unpopular times to frequent the station at Metropolitan Avenue, where if possible he would tag one of the brick walls or the black metal door beside the turnstiles or the repeating concrete pillars that held up the platform roof. His father's brother had gone to the art school on West 57th Street before dying by suicide in the midst of a chronic illness. What most haunted his father was the suddenness of the hurt; he hadn't believed with real conviction in his brother's ailment and so he hadn't taken seriously the idea that directly or indirectly it could kill him. Receiving the call he had screamed into the receiver of the phone. Quinn himself, who had not yet been born, would hear little traces of the sound when later in life his father at the rarest intervals would refer back to that day. His father was sensitive to loud and unexpected sounds, which would make him jump or cry out or both. "Damn it to hell!" he'd exclaimed when his son at the age of seven had thrown a baseball through the plate-glass window of the shop. He had told his son not to toss the ball indoors; he had told him to stay quiet. It was nearly as preordained that the butcher would become a punk as it was that he and his ambitions would be shunted into the position he now occupied, where he cut apart the bodies of animals and wrapped them into sanitized bundles and rang the bundles up so that their purchasers could give him their money and go home. His father cried in the apartment and then, after the couple moved, in the house with the modest footprint.

The girl never seemed to notice that the butcher was now in love with her, even if the days when she would act afraid of him were gone. Once she had come into the shop and had not looked at him with the old suspicion approaching hatred; instead she had smiled and appeared to recognize him although she'd left so quickly that he could see that she still hated the place itself. At the time Quinn had appreciated her new imperviousness to the current of superstition that since his preadolescence had swirled around him. He had also sensed that the girl wanted to tear things up like he did, even if neither of them could manage it. He had seen her, however, as a kid, and that feeling had remained long after she'd grown tall and turned eighteen and started making alternative clothing choices.

After the girl had come back from the musical with the baker and the beanstalk and the witch, which she hadn't been able to resist describing in detail to everyone she encountered, he had realized that they both were grown-up misfits and that she was fascinating. "And I couldn't breathe," she'd said, pausing mid-sentence, "because it was so beautiful." Now thirty-three more months had gone by; now he wondered if everyone else was aware of his feelings, from the housewives with their shoulder bags to their indefatigable children. *Probably*, he said to himself. In his mind he still referred to her generically as the girl.

*

The butcher had the sense that the girl and he would have bonded if they could have talked for longer. Sometimes he would ask her questions only because he wanted to delay her leaving. "How are you?" he would ask, sounding almost tender. "Awful day, isn't it?" It would be hailing or the wind would be picking up and her hair would have been blown around outside, and she would be smoothing it down as she wiped off the soles of her shoes on the mat. He wished he were different so that he could approach her, could propose a coffee date or offer to walk her home or to the library where he knew she went because more often than not there were hardcover books spilling out of her bag when she opened it on the counter to pay for the center-cut steak. He also felt that his taciturnity was what could make them compatible, and the paradox made his head hurt and dejected him although the effect was more pronounced on the days when he didn't see her at all.

He proceeded to exist as usual, which meant cooking at least bi-monthly dinners for his parents in the kitchen where they used to eat every evening. Once a year the dinners were in honor of his father's brother and they would hold hands around the small table where Quinn had laid out the boiled cabbage and bacon and the shepherd's pie and the soda bread marked with an X.

"He had an eye for color," his father would say, rubbing one side of his brow.

His mother would shake her head. "He was loving, so very loving."

"The pottery he made in that kiln—"

Instead of finishing his sentence the father would gesture toward the vase that his son never failed to fill with flowers and place in the center of the table among the four or five platters of food.

"I wish you could have known him, Quinn," the butcher's mother would say.

Always he would shake his head. "I did; I do." Their habit was to let the conversation flow until they began to talk about his father's brother in the present tense. That the brother still existed to them was vital to assert. No one minded that the conversation always unfurled in the same way, like a scene in a play that was so familiar that they no longer needed to rehearse it.

"But you know the sea wouldn't give him a wave," the butcher's father said, laughing, because as insults went this one was affectionate.

Quinn pressed his father's knuckles between his thumb and forefinger whenever his father would let him. He was his parents' only child, which was a shame because he would have liked to read *Bunnicula* to a niece or nephew near Halloween, and because it put so much pressure on him to survive. He would have liked to hold the girl's hand in the way that he held his father's. He wanted to feel the odd, protruding knobs of bone that interrupted her fingers. He appreciated their unexpected shape. He liked that she was uncanny. The bell jangled. "Ciao, bella," he let himself say. It was the most beautiful thing he did between spring and fall.

AN ABUNDANT SUPPLY OF GOOD THINGS

Bice Rappa

Sometimes I tried to say the words in my head at the same time. *Apple. Mela. Pumu.* I tried to say them simultaneously because they had equivalent denotations although they belonged to three separate languages and for me they connoted wildly different things. I failed because although I could twine two melodies together inside my mind like sad-euphoric songs at the end of a rock musical, I couldn't make vocabulary from different universes ring out all at once. Apple was row houses, always row houses, their cross-hatched gleaming pies. Mela was the bible of the neighbor who had read to me when I was a baby and then a toddler and then a small and sullen child. "Percioc-chè tu hai atteso alla voce della tua moglie, ed hai mangiato del frutto dell'albero—." *You have eaten the fruit of the tree*; you know the rest. Pumu was the real apple of myth, coming as it did from the language of folk whispers, where a peasant could marry a king's daughter and she would wake up to find fruits and flowers adorning the room by magic. No, I couldn't possibly say all this together. As a compromise I strung words from the three languages into a single sentence. C'era una volta un pumu, or more precisely, once upon a time there lived una fanciulla, na figghia c'un pumu, always na figghia because where there are fathers in an episode like this, it can be depended on that daughters are never far behind.

This was the summer when I discovered with certainty that my father had been trying to kill me, which was a truth I'd long suspected but hadn't had the wherewithal or the nerve to fully put together. I could have counted in hours or even minutes the long stretch of time that had passed since I'd found out that I couldn't caress the face of a daisy without it wilting. Poisonous plants were fine; I could kiss a bunch of hemlock and it would flourish. People were iffy and survived me if they maintained a certain distance from my breath and fingers. Otherwise they came down with headaches and became dizzy and stumbled around, sometimes collapsing, sometimes throwing up their lunch at my feet, and on occasion it had ended worse. My father had sat on his hands, whistling, pretending not to know why.

But kiddo, my brother would undoubtedly answer. *He made you deadly; he didn't want you dead.* The problem with this excuse is that there is no difference. Because I've done my homework, and the creatures produced by mad scientists—they don't usually make it.

*

I showed up at Gina's door with one solitary backpack.

"You finally did it," she said when she saw me.

"Is your aunt home?"

She shook her head. *No.*

"Can I come in?"

I had to ask because we had barely talked since Gina had confessed to me that her parents hadn't been bitten by a rabid dog and died as she had once tried to claim. I hadn't believed the dog story, but the new version also didn't seem like something that could happen to people outside of fiction, and I was spooked even though I shouldn't have been because my own history was worse. Gina was the first friend my father hadn't been able to keep me from making, and what I had wanted out of my relationship with her was no more and no less than a little joy. My hopes were irrelevant; I was twenty-six, not fifteen, and nothing had gone the way it was supposed to.

The inside air was still hot and stale although the sun was already down. "Tell me," she said. She sat her usual two feet away, her hand on my forearm because she could touch me even if I couldn't touch her.

"He keeps a diary. Can you imagine? My father, the diarist."

"And?" Her eyebrows knitted themselves into a single ridge.

"And he wrote about it."

I paused. "The garden's full of flowers. Poisonous ones. I already knew that. But he planted them on purpose, for me, and somehow—"

I couldn't finish the sentence; she kept on talking as if I had. It was Gina's typical method, this pushing ahead.

"So you confronted him."

"Not confronted. Confronted isn't the word. I asked for an explanation. I gave him that."

"Let me guess; he threw household objects."

"A jar of sauce against the wall. The frozen dinners barely missed me. You know I've been refusing to cook."

"And now you're here."

"And now I'm here." I said it with finality. "I'll get a job," I told her.

She shook her head again. "It's fine. Really, it's fine."

I slept between two blankets at the foot of Gina's bed, which I wouldn't let her give up. A night on her floor was nothing compared to the day when I had seen my father slice open the bird that had died in our backyard after nibbling at the hemlock or the deadly night-shade or the snakeroot. Here I was safe, or safer. In the morning we drove to the closest second-hand store, where we bought me a twin mattress.

*

At first I thought that everything might be okay. Gina brought home a flyer that had been hung with a tack on the bulletin board in the lobby of the library. The company wanted translators, and they hired me and sent me papers in the mail: academic articles about the environmental potential of wind power and switching costs under a duopoly and supercompact cardinals, the mathematical kind. I sat with a dictionary that I used for the more specialized terms, trying to guess the intended meanings of phrases that sounded to me like gibberish because I had never studied any of the concepts they discussed. I started picking at my cuticles again, but I also liked the work or the fact of working, although this is an emotion that I now recognize as irritating and naïve. I typed out the manuscripts and stapled them together and placed them in large orange envelopes that I brought to the post office for weighing, standing back from the counter per usual, avoiding the hands of the clerk. The checks arrived one by one in the mail, and I relished cashing them and then handing the proceeds to Gina's aunt or walking to the grocery store where I would buy logs of pre-marinated pork tenderloin and cans of peeled tomatoes and cheap dry pasta. I hauled the provisions home in brown bags that bumped against my legs as I passed front lawn after front lawn.

We were only eleven blocks north of the address I'd fled from, and they were short blocks rather than long ones. Still, Gina's aunt lived by Juniper Valley Park, on a street where the row houses had mulched yards big enough for shrubberies or were fenced in with pointy white wooden posts that belonged in a picture book. It felt impossible that my father would find me, which is why it was stupid of us to go back of our own accord. We did it because I was tired of borrowing Gina's clothes, because Gina thought we shouldn't let my father have the satisfaction of selling his daughter's belongings. We did it because once again we were bored; being roommates was no longer a novelty. All of this and none of it is accurate, in the way that happens when you're trying after the fact to rationalize a decision that makes no sense.

"We can go tonight," said Gina. Her eyes shone.

"Don't be ridiculous," I told her. "You know he's home at night."

"So what? Oh, come on."

Her voice rose and fell as she prodded and complained. I was just taking what was mine, she said. I protested; she didn't get it. I didn't want to see his face. In the end we split the difference and went the next mid-afternoon, at a time I told myself was close enough to harmless. My father would be using a trowel to remove the mortar from some new configuration of bricks. He would be polishing their surfaces with a wire brush, or overseeing some younger laborer who would polish them. He wouldn't be there. I repeated these affirmations under my breath as we took our usual places in Gina's car, which I drove less and less because I was tired of pretending the city traffic didn't scare me.

On streets like ours where the houses have no driveways, it can be hard to tell when someone is or isn't home. The lights were off and the curtains in the one living room window were drawn. I tried the knob and it didn't give. I fished out my key. Gina followed behind me, loving every minute.

We'd brought a carry-on that belonged to Gina's aunt because neither of us owned a suitcase. None of the furniture in the room where I'd slept had been shifted out of place, but the floor underneath the bed was conspicuously free of dust and debris. It was one of the few areas I'd gotten out of cleaning when I lived there. I started filling the suitcase with sweaters that I wouldn't need for months. Gina had her head in the closet and was flipping from one gauzy garment to the next. "This, this—not this." She tugged the skirts and shorts off hangers without bothering to unclip them.

The light in the house was too bright for the time of day. Gina sang the melody to "Jane Says," the notes getting louder and louder although after the first line she didn't know the words, and the noise was bouncing off the back wall of the emptier and emptier closet. She kneeled down, unexpectedly careful but still singing, to smooth the ripples from a skirt. The door didn't whine and the stairs didn't creak, or if they did we didn't hear them; it was a surprise when we blinked and looked up and a man's head and neck and shoulders were looming over us like they had when I was a child at the kitchen table refusing to eat. Gina and I were both on the floor by the carry-on and it didn't help that I was taller than my father: he was monstrous and dead-quiet, his face red and contorted and I stopped moving. Gina was also almost motionless, but I saw her slip her hand into the pocket where she'd placed a Swiss Army knife before we left her aunt's.

"I'm calling the police," he said.

His feet thudded on the floorboards and the stairs.

"Hello?" Pause. "Police." Pause. "There's a thief in my house."

He didn't say whether he was referring to Gina or to me. I ran, leaving the carry-on behind, not looking back to see what she would do.

*

For the next week I was consumed with the fear that my father could have us both arrested. Gina would crack a joke, rolling over to the edge of the bed and dangling an arm down toward me, and I would try to smile and she would scoff with a disgust that was only half-pretended. She had threatened my father with the knife. She came home later and later from the library until I was already asleep when she arrived and she would have to make her way around me on the floor, nudging the mattress by accident with her foot. She trod on me in the dark. I tried to give the impression of being a girl so asleep that even being trampled couldn't rouse me.

My panic attacks got worse; I would wake in the middle of the night with the darkness of the room lying heavy and expansive on my chest. I stopped being able to concentrate on work. The pages stuck together and my hands sweated when I struggled to peel them apart. Gina called me a drag, a drain on her energy. I was sure she would want me to leave. I had no one to talk to, which wasn't new but was newly painful because I'd become familiar with the opposite of lonely, and I was on the verge of screaming all the time.

One morning I felt myself moving close to that deadened place where you no longer try to exert any control over anything because you've lost your sense that it could help. There was still a small part of me that looked on this possibility with a sense of horror, and I forced my arms and legs to propel me off the mattress and down the stairs swept by Gina's aunt and through the door to the concrete path that led to the street. The birds were out, and as I trudged along I could swear that they were talking. "She doesn't look so hot," they said. "There's one to watch," they said, "and not in a good way." I flipped them off and continued on.

At Met Foods there was only one cart left underneath the window signs advertising Sclafani tomatoes and 24-packs of bottled water. I knew that inside the store there would already be interminable mothers with their children clamoring for chocolate cookies with double frosting and ridged potato chips in bags that made boisterous rustling noises when the children without permission lifted the bags from their spots on the shelf. The mothers were forever replacing items in their original locations or wiping the mouth of whichever child had swiped and eaten a donut. I hated them all and glared with a violence that made me almost immediately ashamed.

The store's newest manager had decided to place a sad selection of bouquets near the entrance, some of which were festooned with ribbons so that when the automatic door whooshed open and hot air rushed in, the strips of fabric would rise up fluttering before coming as suddenly again to rest. Five, six, seven: I grabbed the bunches of roses and lilies by their stems or by the paper they were wrapped in, avoiding their constellations of petals. When I was finished the black buckets were empty except for the water that had been keeping the flowers in a state that looked like life. In the produce section I filled disposable bags with cherries and plums and oranges and nectarines and apples. The apples were red or were a mottled red and green or were yellow and dotted with freckles. I chose them at random and dropped them into the flimsy sacks. They thumped against each other. I filled one, two, three, four, continuing until I thought I might have more than I could pay for or carry home.

Then I waited in line, placing my selections in neat rows on the conveyer.

The pimpled cashier eyed me. "Find everything you need?"

Yes, I told him, everything.

*

"You've lost it," said my only friend.

The lights were on in the room and the room was brimming with flowers and food. I had dug through the kitchen cabinets and the recycling bin under the sink to find the pitchers and water glasses and soda bottles and food-encrusted cans in which the dead blooms were keeping fresh. The bouquets were on the windowsill and on Gina's desk and chair and on the floor around the bed and around my mattress, and interspersed with them were mixing bowls and dinner plates and casserole dishes heaped with fruit. There were the cherries and plums, the oranges and nectarines and apples. There was no space to walk and Gina stood just outside the door, looking blank.

"This is the part where we make up," I said.

Her face was still blank. "I think I want you to leave."

"You think?"

"I do. I want you to leave." The words came out slow and deliberate. She sounded like I had when I'd said I was moving in.

For once Gina's aunt materialized, and she insisted that I take another suitcase and a selection of her clothing and three fifty-dollar bills. On the train I sat hunched over with my cheek pressed against the handle until I could feel it make an indentation on my skin. Although there was a closer stop on the 1, I got out at 96th Street because I needed to breathe. I walked and turned and walked through Manhattan Valley to the new American Youth Hostel, which was large enough for 480 beds, they said, and which looked like a boarding school for English girls. There had been a blackout; the building had already been abandoned and it had caught fire and years had passed before it had finally been refurbished. For five months the hostel had been open to whoever could pay $19 for the night.

They gave me a key and I found my shared bedroom and dropped the suitcase and myself there on a lower bunk. Someone knocked, an employee who must have had nothing better to do, and since I didn't get up to let her in she asked me through the door how I was finding the accommodations. Was there anything else I needed?

Yes, I almost told the woman, everything.

CHECK #164

Luca Rappa

It goes like this. There is a thought that you can't escape, which is something you've always feared would happen and something that has tended to happen because you've feared it, meaning that in theory your current state is routine and shouldn't alarm you—only now it is worse and it does. You've been living in a darkened room, and the sun goes up undetected and doesn't interrupt your sleep, a fact you're thankful for, sleep representing the blessing that it is, the body's grace, and consciousness a knot of sick, of disquiet. The chicken that you eat at midnight is fried but soft and pulpy; it is delivered by a guy your age, a guy with a face that deepens your sense of isolation because despite being intensely recognizable he doesn't know you—"Hey, man," he says late evening after late evening, never varying his expression or tone—and you eat and eat and eat and don't stop to wipe the crumbles from your lips. You are not the child whose dietary conduct your one parent followed with disturbing attention. For good or bad you were left to yourself. Now the specters of all the small hurt bodies in the world are the ones that refuse to quit you. Ghost boys and more so ghost girls invade your brain; whose job was it to deliver them? You can't stop thinking about the things they've seen and the things you haven't. You've been living in a darkened room, and the therapist whose address you highlight in the Yellow Pages suggests a cocktail of daylight and urban running and prescription drugs. You nod back at him, wise and beardless, then make your way to the end of the pier where you attempt to toss the script into the tide. It would have to be folded first into an airplane not to sail back and wrap itself around your forehead. A tide is a thing you've only just learned that rivers can have: they can rise and fall, sloshing against the dam and back like bathtub water. The brain-children crowd and elbow each other, engage in pointless conversations. They are unconcerned with your survival; no one washed their arms or ankles in a vat of suds. The delivery guy comes around again and although you wish you were you are not at home, not figuratively, which is the way in which it counts. To yourself you are a pile of waste, a blunder, a glitch. The brain-children cry in the night.

RAGÙ

Bice Rappa

There were nights when Bice cooked for herself. It would be 12 a.m. at the former Association for the Relief of Respectable, Aged, and Indigent Females, and she would be the only person in the kitchen, which the guests were encouraged to use but which was unpopular during the hours when the bars and clubs were open, and this would be how Bice wanted things: the utensils clinking louder because the kitchen was almost empty, the cooler midnight of a space without bodies except for hers. For a number of weeks she had been alone in a room set up for four hostelers, a room with four metal bunks. Word of the hostel's existence had only just started getting out. Aloneness in a new place was not the same as loneliness and was much better than sitting in a house that was or wasn't yours, waiting for someone you knew and loved to come home, someone who didn't care and wouldn't arrive. In the room Bice ate sauces she had made with tomatoes and beef that were the same as the sauces her mother's mother would have made for large family parties if her mother's mother could have afforded meat, although Bice didn't know this because they had never met and her mother had died too quickly to tell her. What she did know was that the name of the sauces ended with the same vowel as albergu, which was a word for where she was, and agghiu, which was what the sauces needed for flavor, and almenu, which was how most of her more optimistic thoughts began. *At least I'm alive*, she would think. These sauces were made with nutmeg the way a regular red sauce would be made with cinnamon and cloves. The sauces smelled like winter even when it was the end of August and almost Bice's birthday and it was hot enough on the noon sidewalk to make her hair stick to the back of her neck.

When not at the hostel Bice ate where she worked—which, in an incongruous addition to her reclusive life, was the Gray's Papaya at 2090 Broadway. This was as it happened the perfect job for a person who casually secreted poison from her fingertips. She wore hygienic gloves and avoided breathing on her coworkers by requesting shifts with few enough customers that no one else was needed to share the labor. Her bosses obliged without being told her reasons, and there in the shop hung with the sign that read or would someday read *No Gimmicks!*, Bice sold sauerkraut hotdogs and stood on her feet for hours without minding. And she ate hotdogs with sauerkraut, yes, but also with ketchup or mustard or relish or with all four condiments layered on top of each other, and as often as not she paired her food with a papaya drink or with one of its companion beverages because the hotdogs were the saltiest dish for multiple blocks in a city in which that was saying something.

The hygienic gloves prevented Bice from removing with distracted self-cruelty the skin around her nails, and while at first she was bothered by the stillness of her hands in moments when she wasn't passing bags of food over the counter or filing dollar bills in their slots, she appreciated the way her skin regenerated and what this suggested to her about the more distant possibility of other forms of rebirth.

She had flirted with the idea of asking for a job at the restaurant whose owners played opera from the stereo all day, where the back terrace was open in summer and where Yoko Ono was still known to sit although it had been nine and a half years since the assassination of Lennon. "I know you're not hiring," she had planned to say, "but I love this place like everybody does." The sign in the window at the hotdog vendor's had cleared a less complicated path. If by herself at Gray's she could hum an aria or a recitative from behind the hot grill or next to the vat of rust-red onions that she refused to sample even once. "Did you want a drink with that?" she asked over and over, amazed at how her voice sounded like someone else's only because she was talking to strangers and, in a way, enjoying it.

Then she would take off the obligatory apron and the paper hat she wore and return to the hostel, whose new proprietors called her Brenda without being aware that they were wrong. They were letting Brenda sleep there for almost free because in her spare time she was changing sheets and making beds and doing the vacuuming in the rooms vacated by regular guests as well as cleaning their communal toilets. The teenagers on gap years would go out for the night, wearing minidresses and carrying bags shaped like buckets made for children bent on filling them with beach sand, and Bice would return to the kitchen to heat up packets of ramen or, if she had been recently paid, to cook the ragù she'd eat while looking over a new assignment from the translation agency that supplemented her minimum-wage pay. If she was especially exhausted, the three jobs would start to blend together and she would catch herself doodling a mop in the right margin of someone's first typewritten page.

"Oops," she would say out loud. There were women who had lived at the former Association before it had been abandoned and gone up in flames: when it had been devoted to scooping up old widows and spinsters. She had the feeling that they were watching her, the widows and spinsters and her mother, who had also changed sheets and made beds and vacuumed and cleaned toilets but who would have approved of the translating.

*

In November an event occurred that people had been waiting for: rents dropped by five or ten or twenty percent depending on the neighborhood, and on a morning off Bice went looking for a studio apartment. If reading the obituaries with a pen in hand until now had been the best way to find a vacancy, that month the dynamic between would-be tenant and landlord shifted and it became possible to negotiate or, if you were a single girl, just to be taken seriously when you wanted an address of your own without roommates or a boyfriend or a job at Deutsche Bank. With the hazy promise of a fee that might for once be paid by the building owner, the broker brought Bice to a string of apartments in Bensonhurst. The choice signaled that he viewed her as predictable; she considered being affronted. Then the neighborhood rose up around them, and it was complicated because this was a place of histories that would hurt you when you learned of them, but it was also a place Bice recognized and she felt a palpable *yes*.

Which was what she said to the broker over the coffees that they held while standing ungloved outside the caffè with its multicolored flags.

"So, you'll take it?"

"Yes," she told him.

"It's not too small for you? You don't want to look for something bigger?"

"No," she told him.

"Because I do have additional properties. There are some one-bedrooms in—"

"No." She didn't mind cutting him off. "I'll take that one."

The building was prewar even if you couldn't tell unless you squinted to see the pattern the bricks were laid in at its corners, first horizontally and then vertically and in tiny angled pieces that together made little triangles. Bice couldn't have said whether the rents there were cheaper than they had been or whether the broker had sold her a fiction that was only true of Park Slope and the sorts of Manhattan neighborhoods where her mother had polished the black and white halls. The apartment, though, was going to be hers and was therefore worth it and she planned to fill it with an old used bedframe and a drop-leaf table and matching chairs if she could find them, and with the cracked dishes and scratched pots and pans that no one wanted to pay Goodwill for, because she had been saving up.

While waiting for the lease to start Bice sold more hotdogs and scrubbed more toilets, and when that was done she established herself at the communal table in the hostel lobby, where she translated more papers on U.S. hegemony and endangered languages and the impotence of the United Nations in preventing ecological ruin. Once a repeat customer at Gray's leaned over the counter to select a specific hotdog and to ask her if she ever slept. She took three steps back and shook her head and he copied her with exaggerated, teasing slowness.

"Of course," he said, "of course you don't."

Did she know the spot between Grand Concourse and Villa Avenue, he asked, where once a miracle had happened? Then as now it had been fall, and the Queen of the Universe herself had appeared in pink to address a boy in an abandoned lot. Night after night for two whole weeks she had returned and spoken. Bice should take the afternoon, should go and see it. Bice wished the child in the fable had been a girl instead of a boy, but nonetheless she went between shifts and saw the plaque affixed to the chain-link fence and the shrine outfitted with flowers that she couldn't touch, and she was as glad as the broker had made her in Brooklyn and she couldn't explain why. Grand Concourse had been designed with the Champs-Élysées in mind, and the street was wide and airy and since the weather was bizarrely mild Bice decided to walk down to Kingsbridge Road and then to 188th Street although she was following the wrong subway line, the B/D and not the 4, and now she would be late. It was a good sign; on occasion she was starting to relax.

*

After a non-Christmas Bice paid a store employee to move her new purchases into the studio with its parquet floors and shallow tub and blonde wood kitchen cupboards. Careless tenants had nicked and scraped the plasticky countertop with their knives. On the other hand the stove was gas and there were two windows at the side of the space for sleeping that was also a living room, and because of the two windows there was light everywhere, and it was not the disturbingly too-bright light of her father's house in summer.

"Hello, mamma," Bice said.

There were other, larger apartments in the building, ones with multiple bedrooms occupied by parents and their children or by the types of roommates Bice hadn't wanted. The hotdog purveyors had been benevolent and had transferred her to their downtown location so that to reach work she could take a single train from the elevated platform at Avenue P to Washington Square. The route ran above-ground until after the Ditmas Avenue stop, and Bice would look out over the flat roofs of the shorter buildings. She was an enthroned girl on the train, sprawled and gazing, her feet on the edge of the next empty seat. She bought a Walkman and a flimsy set of headphones and listened to the Cocteau Twins on the platform, where finally on January 11th there was snow and it was cold.

Bice noted that she was starting to feel not just gladness but occasional joy. She wasn't surprised when a boy who was her neighbor started following her down 65th Street to the station even though she was going gray and her breasts in the mirror were little lumps. She wasn't surprised when three days in a row on her way to work she saw him in her peripheral vision entering the same subway car she did. *Boy* was the right word; he looked younger than her, twentyish, and was ghost-pale. This she didn't like. What she liked was that his hair was black and his eyes were brown and when he followed her they shone like Gina's. On the fourth day she pretended not to see him when they both went through the last pair of subway car doors. She heard him settle into the seat behind her.

"We're neighbors," she turned and said; it wasn't a question.

"Oh, yeah, um, are we?"

"I'm Bice."

She said it as if she hadn't heard, calculating at the same time the number of feet between them. At least two, maybe three. She waited for him to reciprocate or at least respond. Nothing. She looked ahead again.

Friday, Saturday, Sunday: three more days gone. On Monday they talked a second time, ending the silence of that weekend's awkwardly distanced rides, and in making some comment about nothing he leaned in too close and started showing signs of being about to faint. On Tuesday they were on the elevated southbound platform together at a time when there were no other passengers waiting, the southbound platform because she didn't have to be at Gray's or the hostel and she wanted to see if he would follow her to Coney Island. Next to the sign that read *Avenue P* in white letters, with the lower

Manhattan skyline to his left, the nameless boy grabbed her by the arm and tried to kiss her.

"You're a drug," he actually said as he leaned in.

She shook off the offending hand and began to back away. "I don't think you understand," she told him. "This is not something you fuck around with."

It was tricky. She wanted to keep talking; she didn't want him to pass out. She took a step. He took a step. The tracks were behind her. He was wearing a jacket and so she let herself shove him lightly, in order to put the right distance between them. He stumbled backward, half-laughing, telling her to come on now as he bumped up against the black bars of the railing with the parking lot below. Wrapping his arm around one of the lampposts that periodically interrupted the railing, he hoisted himself up. Then he was sitting on the top rail, still talking and still looking at Bice.

It felt risky, being watched. She was imagining the nameless boy losing consciousness and falling two stories onto the asphalt although she wasn't close enough to make him faint.

"Dude, get down from there. What are you, four?"

"See? We just met and you already care."

"I don't want you to die!"

"So you don't want me to do . . . this?" He was leaning back, his one hand gripping the post.

"You'll crack your head open." She moved closer. "Blood all over the pavement."

"Maybe that's the point."

"Seriously, no more joking; just get down."

She extended an arm. The nameless boy was inches away and she forgot that he shouldn't be if she wanted him not to fall.

She waited. His eyelids fluttered.

Bice caught the nameless boy as he tipped backward, and her arm was around his waist for long enough that she was able to deposit him onto the cement.

*

The two of them could and did lie clothed in Bice's bed in the studio apartment, since he wouldn't retch or become unconscious as long as they didn't turn to look each other in the face. After the episode on the southbound platform she didn't touch him, ever, although they lay and talked about the strange weather and she told him how one day earlier when it was 70 degrees and still winter she had dug a pair of sandals from the disorder of her closet and walked the same number of blocks as the temperature, making her way from their building to Grand Army Plaza, to its fountain decorated with two naked statues back to back. The fingers of the naked woman might have been deadly; the two statues' hands weren't intertwined. Bice continued not touching the clothed boy.

The boy was a fan of Screaming Trees, and "Uncle Anesthesia" had come out and they listened to it by turns through the headphones that felt like they were going to snap as you stretched them over the crown of your head. He termed the song and the band's name appropriate; she was starting to prefer R.E.M. and would sing on repeat about the world imploding, the world helping itself. The last, lowest note would vibrate as she lied a little, again and again. She made trips to Florence Food Center, where they had shouted and cried for Yusef Hawkins and where she bought the same eternal cans of tomatoes and the same ground beef.

"You'd like my friend Gina," she said. "Well, she's not really my friend," she said. Their mouths were occupied, full of the food her mother's mother would have made, for her and for countless aunts and cousins and their children.

Without notice the nameless boy stopped showing up, and soon Bice saw him with someone else on the train: a red-haired girl who threw her head back and laughed, slapping the nameless boy's bare forearm with a violence that said she knew she wouldn't leave a clump of weeping pustules. She'd heard about Bice and was delighted to join the nameless boy in watching her, subtly, as though Bice and the boy had never spoken. Not anywhere or about anything—not once.

HOT WINGS

Martha Lukacs

It wasn't like she always went to the bar and grill that was also a rock club, although this was only because she didn't always have enough money to pay for the drinks and the blissfully spicy chicken while sufficiently tipping the various women at the bar and grill and rock club who deserved to be made whole: not just the bartenders and the skirted and denim-clad waitstaff but also the cooks and the bouncer and the hostess who stood just inside the doorway whether it was March and snowing or March and drizzly or March with a high temperature of 77. In the morning the donor coordinator would arrive for work at a midtown building whose most appreciated quality was its nondescript fluorescence, and there she would check in and screen potential donors and dole out consent forms and salty snacks to approved applicants as well as counsel and evaluate the returners, managing their blood draws and exams and cajoling the more indolent among them into gentle programs of exercise. By the close of business Martha would have been up to her ears in men for several hours and she would be weary, so very weary, and she would often go not from work to home but from work to the bar and grill and rock club because of the relief she felt there.

At first she had patronized the bar because it was where her old roommate had worked in between classes and exams and group sessions at the public university law library whose students booked study rooms a week in advance. Then her old roommate had become a summer associate at Skadden, which had found that it didn't need five names for effective branding, and the roommate had quit her service job and moved out and the coordinator had kept going to the bar regardless, choosing the less busy days and hours when it was easy to ignore the male patrons, even as they distributed themselves across the various leather couches and the row of counter-height stools with backrests, because they would be outnumbered by the women who managed and staffed the place. She needed those Mondays and Tuesdays at 6:15 p.m. because as we've already established, on whichever day it was she would have been up to her ears in men, men who with painstaking entitlement searched for problems to gripe about and possibly to berate her for—who whined as though the clinic wasn't offering a premium for the gift of their DNA.

*

Two days after the year's last snowfall it was April 1st, and there was a girl in Martha's usual spot at the end of the bar that was near the window, and as the coordinator settled herself into the second-best seat the bartender looked at her and the girl and at her again, with an expression that said *Don't kill the new chick; she's okay.*

Before Martha could order her treasured chicken there was a crash that came from the table seating by the bathrooms, and everyone turned their collective heads to see that a drunken boy in a fit of pique had overturned a four-top and with it a pitcher of beer and two plastic cups, both of which had landed in his fraternity brother's lap.

The patron covered in beer was unappealing in a ski sweater and was swearing and wiping himself off with more disposable napkins than any one person had the right to use. His presumably ex-friend, whose chinos were no better than the ski sweater and might have been worse, was approaching the sweater and muttering at it what appeared to be threats. The bartender and Martha and the girl watched as the bouncer tugged at the ex-friend's sleeve. His crewneck's college logo shone under a pendant light.

"Get out," they heard the bouncer say.

"Yeah, get out of here, man." The wet patron was liking being vindicated.

The bouncer shook her fist at him. "You, too." A newer server had thrown down a dishtowel and was kneeling on it as she wiped at the floor with a second rag.

The unwanted customers avoided looking left or right as they slunk by the bar. The door clanged shut and for a second there was quiet.

Then: "What a spectacular display of masculinity," said the girl.

"Earthshattering. Absolute fireworks."

This was the bartender getting into the spirit.

"Remind me why I regret being single."

The donor coordinator felt herself tempted; she took the bait.

"Why do you?"

"I don't like living alone."

"This is a city of roommates," said the bartender, spraying soda water into a glass.

The girl shook her head.

"Adopt a pet," said the bartender undeterred.

"I'm not sure you'd understand," said the girl, "but I think I'd like to have a child."

"Ah, yes. Those consumers of sweet potato, calling for their mothers."

"Laugh all you want," said the girl, who was suddenly serious.

"Some say it's better if you never meet the guy." Martha paused to appreciate her own contribution, which was not quite the same as the pitch they made to prospective mothers on the other side of the clinic, the one its enterprising owner had opened in a nod to vertical integration after a half-decade of record profits.

"You mean, like, a turkey baster?"

"It's called non-sexual conception. Welcome to 1991."

*

She didn't expect the girl to show up at the office, but maybe she shouldn't have been surprised, even though she had told the girl that she didn't handle the portion of the business devoted to people who could become pregnant.

"So, you can help me," said the girl. They were technically closed; the girl had walked in at 5:59. The girl's tone was forceful and ominous and made the donor coordinator think that she'd already agreed to do it, whatever *it* was, and she felt more than a little dizzy.

"Yes, sort of. Someone here can, but not me. And it's expensive."

"This is why I have two and a half jobs," the girl said. "I started scrubbing toilets again for this."

The girl paused. "And what's involved is—"

"Not terribly complex. Some blood tests, an ultrasound. To optimize the timing." Martha was hurrying through the list. "A shot of hCG. Rebecca can tell you."

"Rebecca. Like the film?"

"Yeah, I know."

"I don't like strangers coming near me. Can Rebecca keep her distance?"

In a manner of speaking, she told the girl, yes.

The girl wanted to economize, which meant testing at home for luteinizing hormone without doing a full health panel or the optional genetic analysis, and that was fine because the rest of her health wasn't really the business of the clinic. The girl also wanted a tall, bilingual donor—"no blondes," she said when asked, answering with a vehemence that surprised them. Otherwise she was indifferent, shaking off the clinic's usual questions about eye color and weight and education and religion.

"Then that's that," Rebecca told her. "Call me when the second line gets dark."

Checking after the fact, Martha would find nothing unusual in the girl's chart. *Patient is twenty-seven. Patient motivations for procedure include age, lack of a partner. No previous history of attempted AI. Risks and benefits of procedure were discussed. Patient declines additional testing.* For now the coordinator plodded home, walking slowly so that she could trail five and ten and eventually twenty feet behind the girl, who from the moment she entered the clinic had inspired an unease that hadn't bubbled up when they were talking trash at the bar.

The girl acted as though she didn't know anyone was walking in her wake, and the donor coordinator was just beginning not to think about her when, before disappearing into the stairwell of the subway entrance at 51st and Lex, the girl turned and called out, shouting "Bye, loser!" into the night like they were friends. Like she was trying to be somebody else.

*

They waited for the girl to have her LH surge, and for seven days straight Martha felt antisocial and went to the clinic and back home again to the apartment her new roommate almost never slept at, where she watched a succession of creepy movies in honor of the seven months she had been single. She was in that phase in which you sit around relieved, having embraced the divine blessing that is solitary life, and because this was something she had practiced many times she had become excellent at it, so much so that if you'd asked her she would have been aggressive in telling you that this or that classic film was her favorite, thanks, and that she was more than happy to screen it by herself. She had one of those pillow chairs with arms, which she refused to refer to as a husband pillow like her mother did, the mother's visits blissfully occasional, and she would prop herself up in front of the television and VCR that she had placed on the floor, eating out of a metal popcorn bowl at least sixteen inches in diameter. Endeavoring to cover different sub-genres as well as a span of decades, she worked her way back from a bootleg copy of *Misery* to *The Shining* and *The Exorcist* and *Rosemary's Baby* before ending with that tale of a second wife who didn't care whether her husband had murdered his first one as long as he could make her rich.

Anyone observing the donor coordinator would have seen that she wasn't built for suspense; she had a habit of conveniently failing to pause the film if it just happened to reach a terrifying climax around the time she just happened to need to visit the bathroom. What she really loved was the array of girl and women characters: the crazed fan of a novelist, the twins who didn't care if their appearance made you scream. Would she still love them if she encountered them in real life? At the time this was an open question. She liked to think that she would.

Martha was out on the day when the girl came back, and in this way she missed seeing her until the girl was pregnant, pregnant although it was so early that the ultrasound machine only picked up a yolk sac and the tiniest curl of an embryo. Like last time the girl had come in right before closing, and the coordinator was heading for the door when the girl ran up to her and produced the scrap of paper and said, "Wait—don't you want to see?"

Then the photo was in the coordinator's hand, and she was staring at it as the girl continued to talk.

"You were right. It's better if you don't meet the guy."

The girl's laugh had an edge to it. It made Martha look up at the girl, and when she did she dropped the scrap of paper and they both squatted and tried to recapture it and their hands collided. Now the girl was the one who was staring, and for a moment Martha thought the girl might cry although she composed herself so quickly that it was hard to tell, and the girl and the photo were gone before the coordinator could do or say or see another thing. Her left thumb had started to tingle and she held it up to the fluorescent light, which revealed a cluster of red bumps. They were already suppurating.

"Shit," Martha said.

*

The donor coordinator tested the integrity of a pustule. It was firm and inflamed. Avoiding Rebecca, she dug a Band-Aid from a canister in one of the exam rooms and wound it around the pad of her thumb. Tomorrow she would check the girl's file for clues. She didn't want to do it yet. Instead she left and walked up and over to her building on York and climbed the stairs to the TV and the VCR. She was feeling queasy, and she settled on a home screening of *Bride of Frankenstein* as an alternative to drinks at the bar. In her head she was Lord Byron although she hated Lord Byron, and she murmured his opening line. "How beautifully dramatic!" Martha slid the tape out of its paperboard sleeve. She rewound it. The tape had been viewed before, but not by her.

REUBEN

Gina Puglisi

"It's time," she said. "Oh, love," she told me, "you knew this wasn't for good." *Knew, knew, knew.* The word echoed in my brain like a birdcall. I had been with my aunt for a year and a half, and it was clear that she was feeling an increased nostalgia for her old life—she wanted, for instance, to be able to pad downstairs in her robe and thong for a pint of ice cream and then to be able to eat it lounging on the sofa, without fear of discovery or embarrassment—and it was for these understandable reasons that she wanted me gone. I didn't want to stay in Middle Village without my aunt but couldn't return without a source of income to the city across the water from Manhattan where my parents had raised me. And the Hoboken Public Library wasn't hiring, so the quickest way for me to find a job was to beg to return to my old one.

At the diner Fern gave me a hug. Over her shoulder I saw the manager take in the sight of us. His eyes narrowed and mine narrowed and our mouths were two furrows.

"Wait 'til you see the new menu," Fern told me. "It's perfect. There's a Reuben and paninis—"

"Panini," I said.

"Yes, whatever, and panini and sundaes with flavored syrups that change by the month. The blueberry syrup's made with nutmeg. And brown sugar, and lemon juice. It has bite." She pinched the fleshiest part of my upper arm. "You'll love it."

June would be blueberry. July, mango. August, peach. The manager had left while Fern and I were catching up, and as I drove to the eyesore of a warehouse I recited the litany of flavors. I drummed my fingers against the wheel; I downshifted and braked for pedestrians. I was forgetting the language of my phantom parents, and I couldn't remember the other names of the fruits Fern had mentioned although I knew how to ask for racina, which at one time had been most of what I'd eaten, and alivi virdi, which I so preferred that I would pretend I didn't even understand the words for *black olive*. I thought of my friend, the lethal one. We shared this language but had mostly avoided speaking it; my friendship with the poison girl had been monolingual. Why?

I parked in one of the unmarked spaces outside the building. A roommate was arriving home and we both walked up the stairs. She had groceries on her hip. I took the stairs two at a time for no reason. In the end I still would have to wait for her to let me in.

"I was nice to you," said the manager when the roommate had closed her bedroom door.

"Maybe you tried to be."

"You mean it was a poor showing."

"Yes."

I waited a minute for emphasis. "Make up for it. Ask the sculptor if I can live here."

The manager looked seasick.

"With reduced rent."

He was opening his mouth to tell me no.

"Starting next week."

*

I settled into a cubby that was like the manager's in that it had no windows but that at least featured a raw wood loft for sleeping in. I met the other roommates: the model with a side business designing toe rings and the pianist who was running a recording studio out of one of the larger rooms and the writer whose English expat girlfriend, Feather, was perched naked on the communal couch on the first night when I returned from the diner. "Hiya," Feather said, as if nothing was amiss.

The manager had added running to his roster of occupations and was undaunted by various sorts of weather. He headed out in storms that ended up producing lightning or an inch of rain in fifteen minutes. If it wasn't squalling it was 94 or 96 or 97 degrees, and most of the temperatures were record highs and there he was in shorts that were close to indecent and a pair of wristbands. I kept passing him on the way to the pharmacy or the liquor store and would be unable to resist telling him that 1978 was calling and its racers wanted their gear back.

"It's fucking hot," he would yell. "Pay attention, Gina. None of this is normal."

In my experience this was something that people liked to say. Although the manager had gotten me into the warehouse and secured the discount I'd requested, the tension between us built until a cultural outsider would have thought there was a chance of us killing each other. In the spirit of community preservation I brought a large bottle of gin to the diner before a night shift we were scheduled to share, stashing it in the stockroom until the dead hour between 4 and

5 a.m., when I dragged it out and set it on the counter beside the register, telling him to pull up a stool.

"Truth or dare," I demanded after the first two pairs of shots. It was half a joke; the manager was thirty-six and graying in a way that I imagined made him resemble his father.

"Not playing," he said, nearly slurring his words.

"Fine—just tell me. You know what I want to know."

He was fiddling with a tray that I'd filled with butter packets and individual portions of Smucker's. The butter packets were bent at the corners; this wasn't the first time someone had sat there fidgeting.

"Sometimes I sleepwalk," he said.

"You sleepwalk. That's your excuse."

"I amble down the stairs and out the door. I walk down the street. There are cars approaching."

He was nervous and starting to sweat.

"People honk and stop and shake me until I wake up."

"Oh, come off it," I said; Feather's lexicon was catching. "That's what you wouldn't tell us? You let everyone think I was insane!"

The manager looked down at the unswept floor.

"You think sleepwalking's bad," I continued, not letting him stop me. "I know a girl who's poisonous. Get too close and she knocks you out. Hello, coma. And you're worried about a little somnambulism?"

Here I expected some quick retort; instead the manager stopped mid-sip. "A girl," he said, "who's poisonous." He said it flat and slow, like he was processing the idea, like he didn't think I was making things up.

"Black hair?"

"Brown-black. A little blue in her eye."

"Older than you?"

"By a few years. A lot younger than you, though." I couldn't help it.

"What's her name?"

"Why? You interested?" I laughed. "Beatrice. Well, Bice."

"Oh my god," he said.

"What?"

"That's my sister."

*

Against my better judgment I stuck around while the manager recovered himself.

"Tell me where she is," he demanded. To try to find her he had gone, finally, to his father's house. His father had insisted on referring to Bice as Beatrice. "Who's Bice?" his father had asked repeatedly, perversely. His father had also insisted that Bice was dead. "It's better this way," he had told the manager.

I sympathized. I explained about the hostel Bice had said she was heading to. As I answered the manager's questions I pulled out my knitting. That I could make scarves and shawls and baby blankets out of yarn was a heavily guarded secret. I had knitted after my parents had disappeared, first making a scarf for myself and then producing a blanket that had become longer and longer until it stretched out the door of my rented bedroom into the hallway and down the stairs, where it had draped like a bride's train might if the bride were indifferent to the rancid spectacle of her wealth.

The manager was watching me. "Are you sure you don't want something to eat?" I told him no. I thought of my lethal friend, the scabs around her nails. Not my friend—the manager's sister. I knew how this would go: he would want us to go and find her. The situation was unpleasant and tangled and strange.

I waited for the manager to stop talking nonsense and ask the right question so that I could tell him absolutely not or maybe another time or fine, have it your way. Finally I answered without him asking. Bice might still be living at the hostel; we could pay them a visit. Tomorrow, I said, hating myself.

*

We stood waiting for the PATH train, the manager placing himself so far away from the tracks that it was easy to see how afraid he was of falling onto them. I could observe his behavior and realize without trying that he was picturing his body laid across the rails and the black stones that looked like coal, the heel of his professional shoe caught on a fastener or wedged between two crossties—the look the operator would offer up, seeing him there and unable to stop. My companion was torn between hoping with real desperation not to be crushed by an oncoming train and feeling deeply the stress of continuing to live.

I would have preferred not to notice this because I am not a mystical healer of men and I never wish to be one. "Chill out," I said, stealing from the discourse of uninterested males. It was what they had said at the station across the river from the real city when my mother and my father had been erased. "Chill out, Ms. Puglisi," the men had told me, not bothering with eye contact. My mother and my father would turn up, they'd said. The missing person posters had included wallet-sized images and clipped descriptors and a black and white rendering of the police logo. *Thin build, brown eyes. Clothing: windbreaker.* My mother's jacket for early spring. On the platform at Penn Station the passengers barely moved. On 103rd Street it was 102 degrees. "It's too hot," said the manager. He muttered something about a neighbor. I kept myself from asking.

The woman at the desk was checking in a dozen Parisian hostelers; she didn't want to be useful. They chattered among themselves and about each other, saying "Je m'en fou—" and "Cette meuf est folle!"

and "You've got to be fucking kidding," which we can all agree is most powerfully expressed in English. The woman looked the manager up and down, lingering on the sight of his shoes, and when she asked if she could help us it was obvious what she meant.

"Brenda is a janitor," the woman said.

"Bice," he repeated. "We're looking for a girl named Bice."

"I only know a Brenda."

The woman was counting a sheaf of bills.

I drummed my fingers on the counter. Could the woman check again? No, the woman couldn't. Did we think she didn't know her staff? The woman was sorry, but she had better say goodbye.

The air hadn't cooled when we stepped onto the sidewalk. "Luca, let's go," I said with firmness. "We can come back another day," I told him. "We can ask somebody else."

I'd almost never said his name.

*

The southbound platform at 103rd and Broadway includes a portion that is too narrow for the comfort of even someone who isn't obsessed with death. The best thing to do there is to sit yourself down on one of the wooden seats, which sometimes are decorated with hardened chewing gum or the initials of people who you know must have been young when they carved them. The carvings will remind you that you are old as you sit on the fraction of a bench, keeping your body quiet and bracing yourself for the harsh arrival of the sound: a screech and a rattling that will scare you even more because no one else seems fazed. Once the train is stopped there will be nothing much that can happen, although you could still be caught in the closing doors and the trains that stop at 103rd Street lack a robot voice to warn you to stand clear. What you need is to be vigilant always, protecting yourself from the tracks and the train and the doors and your thoughts about them. This was what I could feel the manager thinking as we stood waiting for the train on the platform so crowded that all the wooden seats were taken, as he pressed his back against the glossy wall.

PART 3: 1991-2010

AQUEDUCT

Agata Costa

We could see where this was going; it didn't take a genius. Not from the night when the girl came home with the plastic bag, the bag stuffed to the brim with bright blue boxes. The walls were thin, and from our individual apartments we neighbors heard the faucet creak and the water flow through the pipe and trickle into the glass, gurgling, after which it would rush down the throat of the girl who wasn't thirsty. We heard the thud of her feet—the girl was pacing and reading a book. We heard the bathroom door close although the girl lived alone and there was no one to see her naked as she straddled the toilet. We could feel her squint as she held the test up to the buzzing light, as she brought it close to her face. The line was barely there. We heard the sound of the one bathroom drawer as it opened and closed and opened. She was lining them up, the sticks side by side or end to end, a store of ephemera that she would keep although she wasn't supposed to, although this defied the definition of the word. Morning by morning we tracked her movements, curious at first, then because there was dread in the air and we didn't like it. The water flowed from the Catskills or the Delaware system into the girl's glass and mouth and then down her throat and into her belly. It didn't matter what the tests had been telling her for weeks; she refused to smile and believe them. The lines appeared and darkened and darkened until they became faint again. We neighbors could have told her what this most likely meant. We could have explained antibodies and thresholds, the hook effect. She didn't ask. We heard the water in the sink and the flushing toilet. We heard her walk the floor.

BACCALARU

Bice Rappa

At eighteen weeks Bice already waddled, and as she moved encumbered around Bensonhurst the world went by with irritating slowness and to speed things up she tried to take in its details. A black Mercedes had parallel parked at the end of a side street where there wasn't supposed to be a car. Now a service van was precariously reversing out of the spot behind the long and fat SUV, was trying to avoid connecting with its bumper and the van driver's companion was out on the curb, helping the driver as he inched along afraid of a collision, of the paperwork that would follow, of losing his job if he wasn't the owner of the company to which the van belonged—she could see the tension in the driver's companion's face as she looked toward the two vehicles, wanting to know that the van would make it out of the space and wanting to express her consternation at the driver of the SUV who turned out not to be inside—and she smiled at the man who was also looking at her and who mouthed *hello* from across the street, smiled so that he would know she was rooting for them, so that he would know that she knew that he knew it.

Pregnancy had changed nothing about her work except that now the smell of the grilling meats made her nauseated and she wanted different foods, which she needed to eat behind the counter without stopping in order to stave off the feeling of queasiness. *Poisonous girls don't throw up*, she told herself like it would make a difference; what did help was not letting five minutes go by together without a bite of salted fish. At home she drowned salt cod in a bowl of water and left it for days in the fridge, changing the water before she left for anywhere and again when she returned until it was a given that the fish's flavor was going to be mild. She put the chopped pieces in a bowl, coating them with egg like a real American would coat stale white bread for stuffing. She tossed the pieces with pine nuts and parsley and too much garlic. She molded the fish into balls smothered with breadcrumbs, then placed them in Tupperware and brought them to Gray's because she liked them best deep-fried the way her job obliged her to fry a corndog.

The crisped balls burned her fingers and her mouth when she tried to eat them quickly, quickly because her stomach would demand it, and her mouth filled up with canker sores that smarted and stung and angered her. But she didn't want to make her stomach or the baby wait, and so she kept stopping off at the market that sold the thickest cuts and eating the balls of fish too soon and singeing the insides of her cheeks and applying Kank-A or the equivalent, tasting the bitterness of the liquid that was not so different from the bitterness of the Red Bull she would someday drink. The fishmongers whispered about her behind her back; the name of the fish was also the name of an indecent word for what they treated as a shameful part of a girl. She tried not to listen or, if she heard, to forget them. "Grazzi, Agata," she would call over her shoulder to the woman at the apartment building who had a key to the studio because while Bice was gone she would come in once more to dump out and refill the water in which the dead fish were swimming. Bice ate the balls of fried fish because they were ocean food and ocean food was in her people's blood.

*

At eight weeks Bice had seen blood in her underwear and had felt so certain that she'd have to return to the clinic and start again that she lay in bed for two days, not bothering to call in sick to Gray's or the hostel although she would need both paychecks to fund another visit. Were the pregnancies of toxic girls classified as high risk? She was taking prenatals but hadn't found an obstetrician. When she was out of bed she was peeing or preparing to pee on a stick, always feeling the silly and possibly tragic indignity of the act. With every test she refused to look elsewhere as the line developed. Was it darker or lighter than the last? If it was lighter, was there an explanation? Had she overdone it with the water? Was the time of day wrong? She would sit on the cold floor of the bathroom, shuddering.

Eventually the bleeding had stopped and, remaining pregnant, she had gotten back on the train. She considered telling the truth to the hotdog emperor and his young wife. *I'm a knocked-up freak*, she would admit. *No one can say what will happen.* No—it wasn't a good idea. They might call the child welfare administration.

The pregnant girl had bought a book titled *Miscarriage* and she read it doggedly, highlighting key sections. When her eyes began to close without her meaning them to, she turned off her one floor lamp and placed the book under her pillow and slept. She wanted a chart that would enumerate her chances of disaster week by week. Not finding one in the book she made her own, scribbling on the back of the last page of a client's list of works cited. The chart was half predictor and half instruction sheet. *Twelve weeks: if you feel yourself move with the tide, your odds are low. Sixteen weeks: beware the maliditti;*

their pain is catching. Loneliness was like inhabiting a blank white space that stretched on and became interminable as you walked it, expecting but never managing to reach the back wall of the room.

She sensed her mother nearby again, but a ghost wasn't enough to satisfy her. Only a person would do. She knew about her mother's miscarriages; her brother had once described them. "Boys rule!" he had said, and by way of explanation he had told her. If she was terrified of becoming her mother she also refused to become her father, which was what would happen if she was really and truly cursed.

At nineteen weeks the blood would reappear. It was pink and monstrous and she wanted to scream at the five writers of the journal article lying on the drop-leaf table, which droned on about attachment theory and disruptive child behavior and which needed translating into hegemonic English. Her daughter could shout *fire* in a crowded subway car, could torture a frog in the shallow bathtub or break into the market at midnight to steal all the fruits from their plastic trays. She wouldn't object; she wouldn't mind. Two inches of rain fell in a day, and it was almost as much as the last hurricane had brought. Then divorced fathers from Long Island to Cape Cod had packed their daughters into rusted hatchbacks, laboring to get them home from weekend visits before the wind and falling trees. Like a rip current the monstrous pink receded and came again. She held her breath like she had in the darkened playhouse. She took more tests; for the moment the line was bright. She tried singing. The baker's wife had also wanted a child.

*

At the hostel they called her into an administrator's office, where the subject under discussion turned out to be her health. She sat, the chair making a noise like the sound of air escaping from a bicycle tire.

"Brenda, are you sure you don't want to take a leave?"

Bice was too tired to repeat her name.

"We'll hold your place," said the woman's assistant, chiming in.

Bice pictured the price tags of infant sweaters and boots.

"Really, we think it's best."

"But here, Brenda, take this." The assistant held out a bag the color of robins' eggs. Bice grasped the glossy rope handles. The bag rattled; she felt weak. She walked out feeling colder than the September air. At the studio apartment she would layer thick tights under jeans and a camisole under a shirt with long sleeves and a boy's sweatshirt that had been screen-printed with a crest and the words PARIS and SORBONNE, which someone had left behind in one of the hostel's unmade bunks. She was aware of its being unhealthy, this wish to either give birth or die. The book was under her pillow; the pink was slow and merciless in coming. She stared at the blank ceiling and the blank walls. She couldn't see the ends of them. The lightness was all around.

BONNE MAMAN

Luca Rappa

I had already determined that Brenda most likely was another name for Bice when I showed up at the prewar building and prepared to buzz. There was a bouquet of flowers in my hand that I thought my sister could admire from a distance, an arrangement rich with carnations and daisies and other species of blooms that reminded me of little girls, and I had asked the people at the gourmet food shop for a gift basket, too, and they had filled it with jams and jellies and toasts so that it looked like it had come from a mail-order catalog intended for the young urban types in my adopted city, and the basket rocked and bounced on my arm as I went up the steps of the stoop.

The hostel administrator hadn't wanted to give me the address that they had on file for the girl they paid in cash and referred to by the wrong name, but I had propped up my elbows on the counter and insisted, telling them I wasn't leaving until they helped me, that I was happy to make a scene. It was a plan of action I'd dreamed up in sleep and so there was a script that I could follow and I had felt relieved at the goodness of the unreal self I was emulating. For the situation I was now in there was no prearranged configuration of words, and as I paused on the top step suddenly I began to fear that I resembled somebody's forlorn and pathetic lover.

Like always I had been running things at the diner, having never graduated with my degree in English although I had just fifteen credits left to earn, the equivalent of a semester, and I thought that perhaps after today I would go home and toss aside the more-than-year-old IPCC report and the unfilled script for fluvoxamine and write. I tried to imagine how good it would feel, knowing I had found my sister and that she had forgiven me. I thought about her as a kid, about the bullies she had cowed and the father whose authority we had lived under. I had seen my father once since leaving. He'd refused to help me find my sister; I had cajoled and shouted and left. I was still at the door. I buzzed.

"Delivery!" I said, disguising my voice. I imagined my sister's look of surprise.

*

The girl who opened the door had silver-black hair and wrinkles around her eyes, and at first I didn't notice she was pregnant. Then I looked my sister up and down. I didn't wait for her to invite me in; I pushed my way past with the flowers and the gift basket and scanned the studio apartment for the presence of a man. Feeling protective and important, I adopted that tone that people use to deliver weighty questions.

"Who did this to you?"

I was acutely conscious of the things I wasn't saying, of how I hadn't accused or berated or blamed her. I was modern, compassionate: the brother she'd been missing.

Then Bice slapped me.

"What the hell are you doing in my house?"

I stood there rubbing my cheek, not pointing out the size of the apartment.

"And where the hell have you been?"

So she recognized me. It was a question that Gina had also asked, and I tried the line that the waitress seemed to have wanted me to feed her.

"I'm sorry," I said proudly.

"I was *nine*," said my sister, her voice low and fierce and resonant.

"I know—I'm sorry."

"Did you know about our magical father? He wakes up in the morning and goes to work pointing bricks. Then he comes home at night and poisons people. And birds: he murders birds. He talks to them and they eat the seeds and flowers and if they turn out to be immune he kills them and cuts them open."

"I only suspected," I sighed and told her. "Look, can I sit down?"

I was fiddling with the leaf of the table, trying to get it to stay extended. My sister and her belly crossed the small kitchen and moved me aside with a shove and in one neat motion achieved what I had been attempting to do.

"No," said the mouth above the belly.

"At least tell me if it's a boy or a girl."

"No."

"Do you have a name picked out?"

"No." My sister crossed her arms across her chest, squeezing each armpit between her thumb and fingers.

"You could name a boy after pà. An olive branch."

"I'm not doing that."

"Is he going to be bilingual?"

Now I had asked a question that she couldn't answer in the negative. The tiny apartment was strewn with dictionaries and thesauruses and manuscripts in other languages than English. There was a typewriter on the table, and its plastic cover lay discarded on the floor in the corner by the second chair that you could tell was never used because of the layer of dust that had collected on each of its wooden arms. I thought of our father's stacks of used copies of *Scientific American*. Why did she have all this? I didn't know, but it seemed genetic.

I wanted to chide her, to remind her of something good.

"I helped teach you to read."

"Time's up," my sister told me, smiling. She was cruel; she was calm; she was relishing the chance to flip the script.

"Let me put them in water for you," I said, gesturing toward the abandoned flowers.

"You want them in water."

"Well, yes."

"Then will you leave? Because if you will, I'll do it myself."

"Is that such a good—"

"I said, I'll do it myself." I watched as she removed the white and green paper, as she unwound the elastic band. Then she threw the cluster of blooms into the sink. She turned on the faucet and looked back at me.

"There—they're in water."

"That wasn't what I meant," I said.

"No shit," said my baby sister. I was still wearing my jacket, and she approached and took me by the shoulders and turned me around until I faced the door and walked me toward it. I wondered vaguely why people kept doing this to me.

"Bye, Luke."

It was my American name. I had a vision of the boy in the coma, and I let my sister maneuver my body out of the apartment and into the smoky hall.

*

Getting out of Bensonhurst required climbing another set of stairs to an elevated platform where in the middle of the night you could wait forty-five minutes or an hour for the train. Gone from the apartment I imagined how differently the experience of discovering my sister could have gone. I could have asked for a glass of water and thrown it in my sister's face. I could have taken a blade from the knife block and threatened her—*Come home with me*, I could have said. I envisioned a messy domestic scene, a neighbor's ear pressed to the wall, a phone call to the emergency hotline.

For a long time I had interpreted these kinds of daydreams as evidence that I was broken. Now I was starting to wonder if I was fine, if it was only the world that was rupturing. There was a little boy on the platform with his mother and I considered what would happen if the mother fell onto the tracks. The boy would be left orphaned; he would have no other relatives. I would take him home to my sister, saying *Here is a child who is like we were*. My sister's baby would have a brother from the start, someone to watch over him. The two of us would raise them both. The train came and went without incident and I didn't move. I wasn't ready to give up this nearness to Bice, to the idea of us living together in a state of something like love. I let three more afternoon trains pass by before I got on one.

*

I'd had the day off because the evening was going to be busy; it was a Friday. The urban professionals came out in full force, girls staggering in drunk on the arms of their boyfriends, to whom they slurred kittenish demands like "Order me pancakes, babe" and "I want a smoo-oo-thie!" Despite being in charge I took orders and delivered plates like I always had, ignoring the instances in which a customer flirted with or insulted me or declined to leave a tip. At 1 a.m. the cook threatened sedition; at 3 a.m. a twenty-something in stilettos bent down and vomited into her purse. This time I had not been near the fryolator. It was not my fault.

When the rush died down and the register was full and the receipt holder was piled high with guest checks, I emerged from behind the lunch counter and let the other staff go and kept Gina back, my hand on her wrist.

"I found her," I told the waitress. "She's pregnant."

Her mouth fell open.

"How did she—"

How was not something I wanted to think about, I told her.

"We're going to live together," I said. "I'll be an uncle," I said.

"I don't think so," said the waitress.

It was pointless to try to convince her. I walked away, back to the register, where I could count and record the dollar amount we were closing with. Gina was shaking her head and smiling a different smile than my sister had, and the source of this smile was something else that I didn't want to understand: why she should be happy for a poisonous and pregnant and lonely girl. But I didn't protest and I let her leave, her bag swinging jauntily like it had no business to, because I was magnanimous and good. I was both of these despite what my sister had said about me and despite the fact that she had shoved me out the door.

I went back home. I didn't write anything in the windowless room. A fellow resident had left half a cigarette in the kitchen ashtray, and I picked it up by one end and relit it and smoked it over the sink. I would go to my father's; he would know what to do. It would be the second time I had seen the house in Middle Village, the house between two graveyards. To make the time pass before going I would sleep and sleep would be a dream, a dream in which I would do admirable things. I had been too hard on my father; it was just the world that was breaking apart.

The next day I woke up and it was like I had been wasted although I had only had the single cigarette. I didn't know what I'd been thinking—I couldn't go to Queens. My sister didn't need me, and I was alone.

JELL-O

Bice Rappa

I couldn't identify the liquid dripping down my leg because I had never been in labor. I was thirty-five weeks and a day or two, and what increased my confusion was that I was not in pain. I had failed to prepare a bag: the duffel filled with pajamas and hot plate and bedroom shoes that the pregnancy manuals advised. I had also failed to prepare a corner of the studio apartment in which the baby could sleep by herself. I'd known that the infant would want to be with me, would not accept being laid down in a bassinet or cradle although I would lie awake beside her because I was sure to fear the possibility of crushing my daughter. Even after my brother's surprise appearance, which I had little desire to think about, I never questioned whether I would have a daughter and not a son.

The liquid continued dripping as I wrapped spring onions in bacon and fried a late dinner on the stove. I counted the contractions that didn't exist. Twenty-five, thirty, thirty-five minutes passed without one. Then I was doubled over on the patch of floor in the open kitchen and the hurt, which arrived like the worst of cramps turned unendurable, made it too late to get organized.

I wandered through the apartment. The prospect of progress felt far-off and I wondered, dimly, what would happen if I didn't leave for a hospital. As a teenager each month I would lie in bed and groan; my father had refused to buy us ibuprofen and the pain would come in wave after wave. Now would the women hear me and come running? One of them could crouch between my legs where my breath wouldn't reach her. Another could cut the cord with kitchen shears. It had been done before and it could be done again. The problem was the date, which rose up before me like a vision; we were in the wrong month. I dragged myself into the hallway. I knocked at Agata's door. I had been living in the building for a year.

"It's too soon," I said, squatting, a towel around my waist.

*

Saying the agony was normal, the neighbor put me and herself into a cab. The driver raised an eyebrow at the sight of the sopping terrycloth that my winter coat didn't cover, but Agata glowered unspeaking at him until he feared what he thought was the threat of u malocchiu, and he sighed and nodded and got out of the car to retrieve and stow away the suitcase she had packed for me. I heard myself make noises that were intermittently quiet and earsplitting and knew they'd both be relieved to deposit me in the maternity ward.

Agata went home on foot. The nurse wanted to know if there was someone she should call: a husband at work, a mother knitting booties by the fire.

"Call Gina," I said without stopping to think.

The nurse frowned. "Is that your sister?"

"I'm an only child."

No one picked up and no one came and the nurse returned the nearly blank address book to the pocket of the suitcase where she'd found it. I was squatting and pacing and curled up and moaning and the nurse was worried. Maternity patients weren't supposed to eat, but I was small and helpless on the bed, like a backyard sparrow that the nurse would have wanted to feed, and she snuck back into the room that buzzed and hummed with machines to ask if I wanted a snack. "Jell-O?" the nurse suggested, referencing a range of flavor options: cherry and raspberry and orange and lime and even blackberry. I wasn't tempted; the nurse didn't like my saying no. She returned with a cup of grapes although this was solid and therefore forbidden food. The cup slid back and forth on the tray as the nurse looked left and right before crossing the hall and entering the room.

"You're progressing faster than we thought," said the doctor when he appeared. He had left me in the room for half an hour. My cries, he'd assumed, were exaggerated, disproportional. Now there was some alarm in the doctor's voice; precipitous births carried a degree of risk. I suspected that the residents were going to be talking about me in the breakroom. I could hear them murmuring. "Her hair is odd," they would tell each other. "So gray, so gray."

The doctor and the multiple other nurses he now called for made bustling movements as they came and went. I had different reasons than they did for being concerned. Being in the hospital was dangerous; why hadn't we stayed home? The baby might be deadly out of the womb. The two of us would be discovered and examined and prodded.

There was still no support person, no one for the doctor to ask if I had changed my mind and wanted them to inject the area around my spinal cord with bupivacaine, and just like that it was determined that on January 26th in the very early morning, with an inch of snow falling to the ground outside, I—the one daughter of Pina and Jimmy Rappa—would give birth without painkillers to a girl named in the language of my parents for the ocean.

"Mari," I exhaled. Then I held my breath.

*

The call to Gina had gone through her aunt, or more precisely through her aunt's answering machine. "You'd better go," she had told her niece, who had picked up the communal telephone at the warehouse. "You know that girl has no one."

"She wasn't wrong," I told Gina.

"You're a mom," she said.

I sighed. "You came."

"Yeah, well, I had to say it."

"Say what?"

"Better you than me."

Then she giggled and I giggled. It struck us as funny, that a poison girl would make a better mother. Somehow, with my eyes half open and my head tilted back, I was able to keep my whole hand on the naked back of the baby. We were skin to skin; the baby was asleep and breathing normally and was full, having had no trouble breastfeeding although the nurses had told me to be prepared, that they had formula for preemies. I'd told them no, that we wouldn't need it, and I had been right.

"They'll probably let you leave today."

It was true; the hospital was overcrowded.

"Are you keeping her away from the nurses?"

I nodded. I knew what Gina was implying. To the army of medical professionals who had decamped after noting the baby's height and weight and unremarkable health, I had only looked neurotic or over-zealous. Gina was wiser; she knew the stakes.

"Do you want me to come home with you?"

Again I nodded. *Yes.*

*

It turned out that the baby was in several ways miraculous. In addition to being the same size as a full-term infant, she appeared both non-lethal and able to withstand me.

"Are you sure?" Gina asked. She had gone out to fetch more grapes, the nurse having ignited an appetite in me that I'd never experienced before. As a child I had felt that I'd had enough grapes for a lifetime, even though I couldn't remember eating any. Now the craving was urgent and I had sent Gina off for a bag of them—"or two, or three," I'd called as she turned to go. Coming back into the studio Gina had seen me dangling a hospital flower in front of the baby's mouth, grasping it gingerly by its stem, and I had held up the unchanged flower for her to see and then, when Gina hadn't understood me, had mouthed the word *nothing* in her direction.

"Shh," I said. I was, in fact, sure—and the baby was showing signs of being ready to sleep.

The feeling of certainty didn't persist. Like I had been afraid of miscarrying, I started to fear that my daughter's signs of being poisonous might come on slowly. I passed Mari to Gina, who had stayed overnight, making her hold the baby to her face. Nothing, Gina confirmed. No dizziness, no flip-flopping stomach.

I moved on to worrying that my daughter's immunity wouldn't last: that holding her bare body would mean producing a necrotic bruise. This scenario disturbed me more. I had retained my prenatal sense that the baby could do no wrong, that I would love her even if she killed us all. It would be worse, having to keep away to save her. It would mean parenting like my father had once we'd moved to Queens and he'd started to keep his distance. My reason would be the opposite of his; he hadn't wanted his monster to make him sick. The effect would be no different. The baby would be left to herself.

I shuddered and resolved to keep cuddling the half-naked bundle as I waited to see what would happen. She woke and slept and drank breastmilk and I sang her songs, trying to regulate my breathing.

"I have to go home," Gina said. She had called Fern at the diner, but Fern's patience had limits. "I have to go back to work."

"Me, too," I told her; my savings were running out.

"I'll call you," Gina said.

"Fine," I told her. "Really, it's fine."

*

Gina understood that there are new mothers who don't want many visitors. She wouldn't share the news with her manager—with my brother, she promised, correcting herself. "Have you heard from Bice?" he would ask. He would pause as if calculating something, then try again. "Did I tell you I saw her?" Yes, he had told her. No, we hadn't spoken. Gina and I planned for her to lie and lie and hoped my brother wouldn't try to interfere and especially that he wouldn't tell my father I'd been pregnant. On the phone at night she told me she was worried; she was losing her appetite for risk. At the same time I think she was starting to resign herself to our connection—that she'd almost have missed it if it was gone.

ITALIAN LOAF

Luca Rappa

Luca was in a corner of the windowless room, and he was sitting and not writing a novel. The novel he wasn't writing was about a boy who'd abandoned his sister. He had been planning the novel in fits and starts but couldn't bring himself to begin to type or write out in longhand the dialogue or descriptive passages or even a summary of the plot. He would feel a disorienting mix of hope and desperation every time he thought of his sister and the book; they could make him a writer and this was what he wanted and even needed both financially and personally, but on the other hand his sister had made him a villain and it was done and he couldn't go back. Now Luca was biting into a sandwich made with week-old Italian bread, which he ate because he felt it was the best he merited although the bread of the sandwich hurt his gums; he felt he had earned no mercy. The blood in his mouth when he bit his tongue was the blood he shared with his father and with his sister and their dead mother whose face had long since started to blur. Luca thought on, and as he thought he picked up the IPCC report and then tossed it aside, and then he thought and planned and didn't write some more. There was something impossible in the idea of his going places, like it would be cosmically unfair to people who were good. It was a stale conceit: he was pitying himself, which he also had not earned. Luca read pages aloud that he hadn't written. "One space or two?" he asked. He could never decide; it was a reason not to start typing. Always the unlined paper stayed the same.

TEA AND TOAST

Jimmy Rappa

What happens to the fathers of poisoned girls? The fathers go to work, driving routes they took the subway to reach before they were promoted, before they were able to buy a car. The fathers sit on the front steps, watching the movements of the residents across the way. One woman rubs the bruise on her leg; another swats a teasing boyfriend. The fathers suddenly begin receiving weekend visits from their sons, youngish men who seem sad and guilty and deluded all at once. Then the pairs of men sit together in the fathers' living rooms, which are bound to be modest and plain but still bigger and more elegant than the ones the sons slept in when they were boys. Then a son becomes liable to interrupt a lull in conversation by announcing "I know where she is"—where "she," of course, refers to his sister: once the object of the old man's violence and now the object of his scorn.

*

"I know where she is," said Luca, and his father replied, "Who?"

Jimmy Rappa was playing dumb. His son made a show of failing to notice, which was the sort of coddling the old man was used to.

"Bice," Luca told him.

"You mean Beatrice," the aging Jimmy said without a hint of surprise. It was a tacit admission that he'd understood all along.

"Sure, Beatrice, yes," the son agreed. "But," he continued, "I know where she is."

"I told you—Beatrice is dead."

"No, pà. She's not dead and you know it."

Jimmy's voice increased to a volume that was as familiar as it was uncomfortable. "I said she's dead."

Father and son took synchronized sips of the tea in which they'd dipped their toast, this being a quaint old habit passed down from one generation to the next and transposed from kitchen to parlor. Now that Luca had started coming around they would repeat the ritual and the conversation an uncountable number of times. Only the existence of the baby remained unspoken between them, and Jimmy sensed intuitively that there was something he didn't know: that they were butting up against some point of no return.

*

Jimmy had subscribed to *Computerworld* not caring that he didn't yet own a PC, and when he was done with *Birding* or its usual alternatives he would flip from one of the magazine's tech articles to the next, absorbing facts about Windows NT and the gender pay gap in information systems and alternatives to data hoarding. For him these facts were only theoretical until one day in 1993 he tumbled headlong into a piece about what then was referred to as doomsday. He read about two-digit and four-digit years. He learned that it would take 14 million hours for a single programmer to fix all the systems that needed fixing. The author of the article didn't mention what its reader extrapolated, which was how water infrastructure and banking services and nuclear and other forms of power would be disrupted by the industry's former fastidiousness about its storage space. Perhaps there would be another war.

The old man began stockpiling food; every trip to the market yielded an extra brown bag or two filled with canned meats and vegetables or dry beans and lentils. He began withdrawing a portion of each check issued by the masonry company. He hoarded the bills under the mattress upon which he had slept alone since long before they had moved out of Little Italy. As even a nominal Catholic he would receive instructions not to believe that life on earth would end with the close of the millennium. By the time the church leaders started speaking widely on the subject he would already be entrenched. Since his wife had died the world had seemed as though it was approaching a terrific finale. Now there was journalistic proof. Most everyone else was unbothered and this was enraging. The IT employees were apathetic; interviewed by newspaper people and by their bosses, they simply shrugged. "By 1999 I'll have left this job and this company," they said. It was somebody else's non-problem, they said. He was the one who knew better.

His son's visits became bimonthly, and Jimmy shopped to prepare for them although Luca would often buy him more provisions while in town. The old man disliked the atmosphere of the larger supermarket; he preferred the littler stores that could fit in a single corner of a small building. Even better were the ones whose proprietors sold a single category of food. The butcher was younger but a pal nonetheless, in Jimmy's eyes a favorite although some of his questions were unwelcome. "How's that kid of yours?" the butcher would ask when his customer walked in the door. Jimmy would fail to answer and the butcher wouldn't follow up. Father and son were going to bond over the frying meats. They would sit at the round kitchen table and saw through the steak made tough by the process of overcooking it on the stove. The sawing made the act of eating as grisly as it would have been if the meat had still been bloodied and red.

As they ate Luca would try to convince his father of the actual dangers they faced. One fall morning he broke out and waved around an excerpt from the IPCC report, the chapter on time-dependent greenhouse-gas-induced climate change, whose twenty-two pages he had begun rolling up and tucking into his back pocket before he left the house.

"Give me that," said Jimmy. He had another use in mind for the twenty-two pages; a fly was buzzing around the table.

*

That November it came time for Jimmy to retire, and the masonry outfit organized a going-away party for the employee who had worked his way from gray mortar around the borders of his fingernails to an office with its own four walls and glass-paned view. At the party he returned and returned to the punch bowl, sloshing the pink-red liquid messily with the ladle into a translucent cup. Rivulets of the sweet beverage made their way down the side of the cup; he dabbed at them with a napkin. The napkin looked, before it landed in the office garbage, like the paper the butcher would wrap around a juicy cut of meat. The aging Jimmy moved from one group of chatting coworkers to another, singling out the groups with younger women. "Having a good time?" he asked the receptionist with the remote stare and the houndstooth blazer, whose waist he attempted to encircle with two arms. The blonde shook him off, saying "You silly old thing!" like it was 1961. Rather than leaving alone or with a final bonus check, he departed carrying an annual all-access pass offering admission to the Beaux-Arts-era house and the Italian gardens at 119 Vanderbilt Park Road. The house and gardens had been established by a rich

American capitalist who in daguerreotypes had sported an aggressive handlebar mustache. The rich capitalist himself, ironically, had never retired. *Because we know you love your plants*, someone had written by hand inside the card in which the printed pass was nestled.

It would take an hour and forty-six minutes to drive from Middle Village to Hyde Park, and when he reached the town of Hawthorne Jimmy stopped off at the Sunoco station, a squat white building with two gas pumps and a selection of scratch-off lottery tickets behind the counter. For the first time in his life he asked for the silver and blue and Creamsicle-colored tickets by name. Sitting in the driver's seat with a penny between his thumb and forefinger he scratched and scratched. The little flecks of gray landed on the floor below the steering wheel. He stared down and swung open the car door and re-crossed the stretch of cracked asphalt that lay between the pump and the door of the squat white building.

"I think this is a winner," he told the cashier, who was bespectacled and wore a bucket hat pulled down over his forehead.

"Looks like it," said the cashier.

"Beginner's luck," said Jimmy Rappa.

The cashier licked a finger and with the finger proceeded to remove from the register a succession of bills.

"Let me give you a tip, young man," said the recipient of the wad of cash. "Rough times are coming."

He leaned conspiratorially across the counter. "You're going to want," he said, "to be prepared."

Then he returned to the car and did a three-point turn and pulled back onto the two-lane road. Instead of driving the rest of the way to the Beaux-Arts-era house with the Italian gardens, he took the parkway south again to Queens, whizzing by the Gate of Heaven Cemetery and the Kensico Reservoir with the bills burning a hole in the pocket of his pants.

*

Jimmy on an errand was to himself a model of contemplation, the beneficiary of an observant eye. The neighborhood was crawling with boys on bikes, boys who could have been eight or nine or ten, and as he drove and parked and then walked he was thinking of his son before and after the demise of his wife who had fainted and talked of voracious babies in her belly.

Had the babies liked grapes or plums? The fruit had been purple on the outside and a lighter color on the inside. He had hoped for a living daughter; then his wife had died. The chemical smell had followed her home. Or maybe it had been the girl born in the one bedroom who had killed her. That would make it the fault of the person who had wanted the infant. No—he preferred to imagine Pina murdered by her employers' largesse, the chemicals doing her in. His daughter he had wished to shut away, protect. With food, with plants. If she ever had a child—

Before he could complete his thought the door of the shop on the corner appeared in front of him. He went in; he took out the wad of bills, which in the previous week he had decorated with a new gold-plated clip.

"I'd like two dozen boxes of ziti," he told the shop assistant. "A dozen cans of plum tomatoes."

Here he paused. "A case of green olives, four bulk-packs of cornflakes." The cornflakes were his most recent concession to the rhythms of U.S. life. He could envision, if the house's refrigeration failed, eating the toasted mouthfuls with no milk.

"Five pounds of enriched flour," he said. "And a dolly to load them onto."

The shop assistant looked at him suspiciously; the old man wasn't a business. "Why a whole case?"

"My children these days have quite the appetite."

"You'll have to special order."

*

It was a choice when, rather than stacking the goods in the basement of the house on 67th Road, Jimmy Rappa let them pile up in the house's entryway where he and any guest could see them without trying. Already there had been the accumulated mound of grocery bags filled with lower-quality items: the canned meats and vegetables and the uncooked beans. To these he added the boxes of ziti and the cans of plum tomatoes and the jars of olives and the plain brown and white sacks of cornflakes and flour, respectively.

"What is all this?" said the son the next time he arrived at the house. Luca wrinkled his prominent nose. The bags had begun to encroach on his walking path; he'd had to move some of them aside to pass fully through the entryway and into the kitchen with the hideous tile on its walls. A hole in the corner of one of the brown bulk-packs had attracted a cluster of ants. Jimmy still obsessively cleaned the six bedrooms, but he didn't clean the spot that the goods had overtaken.

"I stumbled into a little windfall," said Jimmy, ignoring the moving insects. "We'll be ready for anything," he told his son.

The son started to speak—the father put up his hand. He took his visitor's beige overcoat.

"Now, figghiu," he said, approximating tenderness, "come and have your tea."

TWO STEAKS

Bice Rappa

Meanwhile there was Jimmy Rappa's daughter, who was still in Brooklyn, and his daughter's daughter, who was still miraculous. Ten days after her birth all the infant's swaddles had needed washing and she had cried so hard in protest that Bice had also cried and laughed and shouted, not to frighten her but to commiserate, and they had both wailed until the water for the bath was ready and then quieted themselves as the new mother plopped them into it and they discovered that the water, being hot, was just as good as a piece of cloth. While sleeping the baby would raise her arms and pucker her lips; she was in bed with her mother and was happy enough to rest.

Bice went back to work at the hostel, whose administrators had tried to encourage a longer leave. When appealing to them she had brought the baby so that they would have to face her, would have to imagine mother and daughter running out of cash. Once the administrators had relented she kept on bringing the baby so that mother and daughter would not be separated, and she wore her facing inward and narrated the work in detail—"Now I'm scrubbing the inside of the bowl with a brush," she would say—or else she sang folk songs from a used cassette tape she'd picked up at Downtown Music Gallery. The songs had been written and sung by a man who had died at thirty-three of smoke inhalation in a fiery plane crash. She had fallen in love with the more haunting of the melodies and chords, which somehow still managed to telegraph a sense of joy, and only later had learned the sad story of the plane. She refused to give up the songs or to interpret them as omens. She was working hard to believe that nothing would happen to the infant, who gave no indication of being weak or delicate or lacking in conviction.

*

Around the time of the baby's first birthday Bice felt an undeniable and illogical need to go to Middle Village. She missed the house where she had lived until the day she'd discovered her father's journaling. She missed walking by the cemetery although she had never gone inside the gates after the incident with the flowers. She missed driving slowly past its gravestones in Gina's car on the way to or from the movies, and it occurred to her that maybe it was really the carefree Gina that she missed or the age they had been—but she also had been thinking of the butcher and had found that she couldn't stop. She wanted to know what had become of him, of the shop she had gone to almost every day.

This happens to mothers; they want to feel they are from somewhere. For a daughter of Jimmy's it was bizarre and even dangerous, this pull toward a place that had hurt her. She feared intensely that her father, no longer having someone to run his errands, would be in the shop when they arrived. He would trail them to the studio apartment although the trip on the subway would take over an hour. He would pick the lock after nightfall, entering the apartment to poison the infant he would call niputi: to poison or seize her or both. "You're being silly," she told herself in the mirror, talking out loud for emphasis. Her father had turned seventy-three the year before; there would not be much he could do. She was entitled to a past, to surroundings she could narrate to the baby other than the sights and sounds and smells of Bensonhurst and of the supply closet at the hostel where the baby still guzzled breastmilk.

Soon it was spring again and the baby was now a toddler and was also eating avocado mash and gorgonzola from a tiny plate. This was the year when a chef in Australia would claim to have invented the open-faced sandwich buttered with the electric green fruit. The toddler appeared to like chewing mush and Bice obliged her, spoon-feeding her between hours spent with Dr. Sears, whose new book had a cover that matched the hue of her child's lunch. As May wound down the toddler began to earn that name by walking. Over the summer there were beach trips during which, decked out in a ruffled and dotted swimsuit, Mari squatted and dug in the sand that was safely beyond the water's edge. Bice was forever filling the bucket with water and bringing it to the toddler so that the toddler wasn't tempted to approach the tide, although she was bothered by the way that filling the bucket required leaving the toddler for an instant or two or three. The specter of Jimmy Rappa loomed. Still, Bice told Gina about her idea of returning home, of bringing Mari there. "For a kind of tour," she said. "You're crazy," Gina told her. "I'm not condoning this."

The end of the call was amicable, and the barely new mother sat and sat with the pull she felt toward Middle Village until at last she decided they would set out on the underground journey that would bring her and the toddler back into Manhattan only to spit them out in Queens. Some days that autumn had been balmy; on some mornings the temperature had reached a low of 34. She packed the toddler into a snowsuit although the skies were clear and the snowsuit into an umbrella stroller that was still too big for the squishy body she grasped in her hands.

*

The butcher no longer hung dead pigs from their hooves in the window. With time the buying patterns of his customers had revealed that the whole carcasses were too gruesome a decoration; no one wanted to think about what they were planning to buy and cook and eat. Otherwise the shop was unchanged when the no-longer-new mother wheeled her toddler in through the door whose bell jangled as she opened it. The butcher was reading the new King novel, which had been written without chapters or section breaks and whose structure made interruptions especially annoying. Bice would have liked the book if she hadn't always on principle avoided narratives of horror. Its protagonist was a maid like her mother, the dust a menace but also a constant companion.

"Ciao, bella," the butcher said, his whole face lighting up. He was still not from the island where her parents had been born.

Bice felt herself smile.

"One steak?" he asked her.

"Two," she said. The toddler would eat right for her blood type, which was B negative, even if her mother had to puree the meat into a pulp. The toddler wouldn't turn anemic under her mother's eye.

The bell jangled again as the door creaked open. Bice stiffened. She was a child receiving a neighbor's hug; she was a child at the kitchen table.

*

Here is what Bice didn't know: "We're out of meat," the old man had said that morning.

"I won't have time," her brother had told him. This visit had fallen on a Sunday and the interval between trains was even longer than advertised, and if he wasn't careful he was going to be late for an afternoon and evening shift at the diner.

"I'll go myself," her father had said.

He hadn't been angry; for this Bice's brother had been grateful.

Luca had taken his overcoat from the hook by the door and had put it on and walked quickly to the station, quickly because he was already further behind than he'd wanted to be. Bice's father, in contrast, had taken his time, walking and turning his head from one side to the other as he took in the sights of the neighborhood.

*

The no-longer-new mother forced herself to turn in the direction of the bell. The stranger who had opened the door was not a man, was not old. She was a woman with two children, a boy and a girl who crowded into the small space, shoving each other and talking at a volume that was better suited to the sidewalk outside than to the shop where the butcher had been hoping to read.

Bice exhaled. "Goodbye," she said, quickening her pace. As always she had taken the wrapped packages without touching the butcher's hands. She reversed the stroller toward the exit, navigating around the boy and girl who were still lingering there although their mother had approached the counter and was starting to order the meat for three days' worth of dinners for five. The oldest child was at school, she told the butcher. "Have a nice day," Bice called, her voice overlapping with the other woman's. She tried to sound sweet and unconcerned. She and the stroller and the toddler turned a corner. She wondered if, as Gina might say, she was losing it. Middle Village by now was home to 30,000 people, people who referred to their place of residence as a town although technically it had always been just a neighborhood.

*

Bice's father turned a corner, too, and he entered the shop. "Ciao!" cried the butcher who was not from the island. "I've just seen your daughter," the butcher said. "And the little one."

His fingers made a chef's kiss; the little one was scrumptious.

The old man blinked.

*

They walked and walked and reached the station, which had no stairs, and Bice with practiced urgency plucked the toddler out of the stroller and collapsed it and carried them both through the turnstile and to the platform to whose very end she walked, still not putting either of them down, so that if anyone wanted to find or confront them that person would have to go as far as possible before reaching the spot where they stood.

She turned and looked around; she tapped and tapped her foot. The trees were bare. The train approached and squealed and slid into the station. They boarded—they stood clear of the closing doors. She settled them onto a pair of seats, still scanning the half-empty car. There didn't seem to be any impending danger.

SPAGHETTIOS

Gina Puglisi

A call didn't come from Bice and Luca's father on the shared wall telephone at the warehouse or the diner. Instead he waited until his son returned to the house on the third Saturday of the month.

Entering the kitchen Luca noticed that his host was silent, that he didn't look up from his toast. They both waited a beat or two. Finally his host began to speak.

"You didn't tell me about the picciridda," he said.

"No," Bice's brother agreed, confessing to him like—years later— he would also confess to me.

*

Mari was three feet tall and was standing in the kitchen of the apartment near Avenue P, and you could tell from her expression that she was listening to everything we said. The conversation between her mother and me had involved premonitions and cajoling but so far hadn't resulted in Bice poring over the Town and Country Properties section of the *New York Magazine* issue that I'd bought her, hoping to argue convincingly that it was necessary.

"You need to get out of Bensonhurst," I said.

"You sound like me. Where is Gina? Where's my daredevil friend?"

"I'm telling you, you were right—they're planning something."

"Did he tell you that? What did he say?"

"He didn't have to, Bice. I can feel it."

"You can feel it. Listen, I've been down this road. I went to Middle Village. I was scared and I went there anyway. Did I die and no one told me? Are you talking to a ghost?"

"That was once. What about next time? Think about it: Luca tells him you're a mom. They show up here together. They want his grand-kid. Think about what happens."

Mother and daughter needed to move, I insisted. Maybe to a different city; maybe to a different coast; at least to a different address. I shoved the copy of the magazine into the hands of my poisonous friend.

I use the word *friend* because since Mari's birth I had gradually thought better of my plan to separate myself from Bice. I may not be a mystical healer of newly anointed managers, but there was something about nursing her postpartum—about emptying the bathroom wastebasket and cooking her diner-style eggs and buying her fruit from the corner store—that appealed to my sense of justice. This girl deserved for once to be properly fed and cared for, even if she was the cursed daughter of a woman named Pina and I worried that like Pina or like my parents she would disappear or die.

*

On the four-year anniversary of our encounter in the library I proposed, for old times' sake and as a form of celebration, an outing: we'd go to see a band play ninety minutes south of the waterfront city I'd come back to.

"Think of it as a test run," I said, still working my angle. Bice could get a feel for what it might be like to leave the outer boroughs, to embrace a location that was technically two states away.

"Driving isn't good for our relationship."

I thought of my car's open windows, rain dribbling onto the ruined interior. "Fine," I said. "We'll take the bus."

The neighbor Agata was called on to watch a sleeping Mari, first while we zipped ourselves into tight outfits and then while we exited the building. Bice was wearing a bootleg copy of the Whaam! dress that featured appliqued steam trains and a rotary phone. My dress was black to match a pair of combat boots and was slinky like pajamas because otherwise I would be uncomfortable on the ride back. If we had been heading to Jersey we would first have had to make it through the bowels of a drab and brown station, which you entered via an escalator from the street and where the crown jewel of the various food and beverage stalls would one day be an Auntie Anne's. The only place worse was Port Authority. Its bus berths were menacing in the yellow light, but no one took the train to Philadelphia.

"Here we are," I said as we settled in. Our seats were rainbow-upholstered; the places in front of us weren't taken.

"Wasn't the idea," asked Bice, "to keep her safe?" Although Mari was two years and seventeen days old, she had almost never been separated from her mother.

"Think globally," I told her. "We're getting to know a new place. A place where you'd be untraceable."

"I don't like cheese steaks," said the mother who couldn't afford to be choosy. "Philly," she said, sighing. "Land of belligerent drunks."

*

In another fifteen years the Trocadero would be closed, its doors boarded up and speckled with the white remnants of peeled-off concert posters. On that February night they were hosting a band from Manchester whose most pervasive international hit was a song that couldn't be run uncensored on American music television because its descriptions of female pleasure were too explicit. The band's frontman sang under the late Victorian proscenium arch about a girl who thought she was wild and crazy. I didn't especially like the band but had decided that they would do. The lighting designer had embraced a Britpop vibe, and the sea of shadowed faces in the standing-room-only section below our balcony was awash in fuchsia. I glanced at my friend and she was a marvel: eyes closed, hands up, like she'd forgotten I was next to her. I lay my head on her shoulder during a break in the setlist. We walked arm in arm down the stairs to the bathroom on the ground floor. We sat again in the balcony's front row, Bice lounging, wedge heels clicked together and her chin in her hand.

Then the light changed and I looked down and thought I saw him, leaning against a gold-green pillar. Shock of black hair, unhip shoes, with a face I could only see in profile. I turned my head again toward Bice, whispering.

"Is there any chance," I asked, "that your brother could be here?"

I pointed; she stared.

"In Philadelphia?"

I made a gesture of confusion.

"Did you tell him we had tickets?"

"No! Did he follow us? Why would he be following us?"

My poisonous friend squinted again, and I could tell she wasn't wearing the contacts that she'd discovered she needed in order to see from far away.

"It's not him," she said.

The frontman was singing the opening lyrics to "Out to Get You."

Younger girls than us were swaying along with the plaintive guitar. I watched as the shock of black hair and the unhip shoes moved back and forth. The person who might or might not be Bice's brother was restless, almost pacing; he was looking around.

I couldn't articulate what I thought he might be planning, but it was the second time I'd suspected the manager of trying to pull one over on me.

*

Our journey home by bus went on forever. We had left before the end of the second set, looking over our shoulders every block of the four-minute walk to the station. If someone was still in our wake he was hiding it well, keeping a clump of other strangers between us and him. I felt safer when we were on the bus, but only slightly; I scanned the other rows of seats as if it were possible that he could have overtaken us and arrived there first. It was freezing cold and we shivered in our short jackets. I leaned my head against the window instead of on Bice's shoulder, and as the bus took curve after curve I noted that the glass, which had come loose from its frame at the bottom, was swinging outward toward the edge of the road.

"Centrifugal force," I muttered.

The frigid air leaked in.

"What?" murmured my companion; she was dozing off.

"Nothing." I craned my neck and again I looked behind me at the rows of passengers in dark clothing, at their ghostly disembodied heads.

When we turned the last corner before Bice's building, we saw the street blocked off and lit up like a supermoon was out. "What is it? What's wrong?" cried Bice, and I knew she thought there'd been some catastrophe involving Mari, whom she would never want to leave at home again.

"Get out your glasses," I laughed and said. At the other end of the block someone was shooting a film scene. "She's fine," she breathed as we entered the kitchen, the two-year-old asleep holding Agata's two hands.

*

Female Roommate Wanted—For lrg 2-BR apt on 4th Ave. Quiet nonsmoker; no pets. $370 plus utils. Refs required. The advertisement had stood out because its writer's lack of an animal companion had suggested that she wasn't warm or cuddly, that she wouldn't want to get close. The writer of the ad had asked for quiet; maybe she would be standoffish and barely talk to them. She might heat up SpaghettiOs in the microwave on an undecorated kitchen counter with no intention of eating them in the shared living space. She might take the bowl into her room, eating the meal that could barely be classified as pasta at a scratched-up antique desk. Yes, these possibilities were attractive, and I made and remade my pitch until Bice called the number that had been included at the very end of the ad. The writer proposed to meet the mother and the daughter, the daughter who that afternoon in Prospect Park was so silently observant that the woman agreed to let both of them move in. Together they would qualify as one unobtrusive tenant.

Bice and I decided that if she refused to leave the state then a double layer of protection was desirable, and to achieve it we plotted to make her male relatives believe her intended destination was California. "I'll tell Luca I saw you, that you went to Santa Monica," I told her. "I'll make him believe it," I promised again. "You didn't leave an address." I was spending more and more days off at the studio apartment, drawn in by Mari, whose clinging body I would carry around while her mother crammed belongings into boxes, until my arms gave way. We still didn't know if it had been Bice's brother at the Trocadero. I didn't confront him, didn't ask when we were both at work or at home.

Even after the move, mother and daughter still went every day to the hostel whose administrators had promoted Brenda to lead housekeeper and continued paying her in crisp twenties. Mari had a toy dustpan and broom, and she gathered up pretended chunks of dust and hair and decomposing insects in the pan while my friend scrubbed and swept away the real debris. At night Bice continued translating the academic papers, whose finished English versions I would sometimes pick up and read if I was bored. They had increasingly often to do with the climate crisis and infectious diseases, or the climate crisis and the layperson, or the cost of slowing a climate crisis down. It was the only work she had been able to do while recovering from childbirth; the translation agency had never even known that she was pregnant.

STOLLEN

Mari Rappa

At five years old Mari stood on top of the kitchen table in the shared apartment and danced. It was December and she and her mother had been eating stollen and listening to public radio. The live singers were performing a song in Catalan, a song about a river, and the song moved her more than the carols that referenced rooftops and platinum mines and donkeys with absurd faux-ethnic names. *God has kept the wolf from our lamb*, the choir sang. For now the lie had kept the wolf from their door.

That September had meant the start of school, and the little girl's first-quarter report card had come back typewritten on onionskin paper. The report said that the little girl was precocious, that she talked too much and too loudly. She was not like she'd been on the day in the park with the roommate. The kindergarten teacher hoped to witness future growth, that the little girl would *give others a chance to speak*. The school was on a street that shared its name with a cheap property on the Monopoly gameboard. The little girl badgered her mother; could they play the game after work? Her mother never said no, even if she had a headache, even if she had more papers to translate after the little girl went to sleep in their still-shared bedroom. Instead Mari's mother selected a token, the thimble or the shoe, and lifted it and placed it delicately on the multicolored board. Instead her mother rolled the dice, which hit the board with a thwack that satisfied them both. The little girl laughed; the mother took her hand. It remained miraculously possible to do this. Mari was quite happy despite being misunderstood at school, despite being written about in ways that made her mother spit out swears under her breath. "Minchia," Bice had said in reference to the report card, ripping the onionskin sheet to pieces over a stinking can of kitchen trash.

*

The following March the little girl was six and it was 86 degrees, and she was hustled into a dress and patent leather shoes that stuck to her feet and squeaked. Both dress and shoes were used but had been carefully chosen, and Mari shuffled down the sidewalk with her mother to the Atlantic Avenue stop and then to the theater where they saw a show her mother had saved for months to afford. The show was not an obvious choice for her mother because it featured a family of children in danger who to save their own lives would need to flee an approaching villain, and because her mother did not like books or plays or movies that hit too close to home. They sat together in the darkened hall, the mother as always grateful not to have killed anybody yet, the little girl enraptured and already sure she wanted to be a singer.

"We'll see," said Bice at intermission, clearing her throat.

After the play Mari was sweaty and her mother washed her skin off in the tub. She splashed the little girl's bare back with water, tracing the intricate pattern of dark hair that sprouted between her shoulder blades. Mari didn't have her mother's blueish eye or the white hair on her head, but the pattern of body hair was familiar, and so were her lips and cheekbones and the rest of her face.

In personality Mari was more distinct, recalling a former child actress from the last show the two of them had seen. The production had been put on to mark the tenth year since the opening of the musical about the baker and his wife, and Mari's mother had taken them there to introduce a lesson. That day the little girl's attention had been drawn to the former child actress, who had been wearing a red cape and had not been afraid of the wolf disguised as an old woman. Leaving the theater Mari had tilted her chin up and looked at her mother and then had spoken in her usual loud voice, saying "Mamma, why don't you have a husband?" During the ride home mother and daughter had talked about strange men; the idea was not to be foolhardy. A little girl should never trust such men, they'd finally agreed.

On the hot night in March the little girl lay nose to nose with her mother and the overwhelming love they both had gotten used to.

*

Here is what Mari didn't stop to consider: her mother hadn't just sprung fully formed into being without parents. Journalists had started covering the looming technological disaster and had given additional ammunition to the little girl's grandfather, whose house with its impossibly small bedrooms would be piled high with bags upon bags of non-perishable goods before she realized he existed. There were hundreds of bags now, bags filled with logoed and multicolored items he had never even bothered to unpack, and he stacked them on top of one another and leaned the stacks against the walls and corners of the bedrooms so that they wouldn't fall over. Now the rooms lay mostly undusted and some of them were full to bursting.

Mari's uncle hadn't ceased visiting the house in Middle Village once he'd discovered that he had to move the bags aside to pass through the entryway and into the kitchen with the disastrous wall tile, much as he hadn't stopped himself from going there after learning for certain or almost for certain that his father was a poisoner, and much as he wouldn't stop visiting once the clutter expanded to fill the other rooms. He had spent nights loitering outside the Bensonhurst apartment building, watching mother and daughter. He had made a pledge to Mari's grandfather that he would do this. For the picciridda, they both had said. Then the little girl and her mother had disappeared, had turned the tables, and everyone else who could have been his family was buried and gone. Now he was stuck stooping to clear a pathway toward the linoleum that was the filthiest it had ever been. He refused to take tangible steps to find Mari and her mother in a city where he no longer believed them to be living, although every so often he halfheartedly pumped Gina for information: "Has she been in touch?" "Have you heard anything?" Each time he repeated himself, only changing individual words.

To Mari's uncle it felt interminable: the time that went by between the Sunday when he hadn't gone to the butcher's and the day when he gave her grandfather the name and address of the youth hostel. Someday Mari would tell herself that he had meant well, that he'd believed he was being rebellious—*Find her yourself*, she pictured him saying in anger. Maybe he'd considered calling the hostel administrators after the fact, relating the story of domestic abuse. *If you know where they are, please don't tell him*, he would have had to say. *And please, don't tell me either.* It was true that the little girl's mother had given the hostel their new address, that their roommate on 4th Avenue was her second emergency contact. Either way her uncle never did pick up the warehouse or diner phone.

POISON CONTROL CENTER

Jimmy Rappa

The pawn broker barely raised an eyebrow when the old man requested to see the pearl-handled semi-skinner knife and then the commemorative sword fashioned in honor of a moon landing and then the Smith & Wesson stainless steel handcuffs manufactured in Houlton, Maine. The prices were steep, but like the cash from the Sunoco station had done, the monthly proceeds from the pension administered by the bricklayer's union continued to burn a hole in the pocket of the handmade pinstripe trousers that Jimmy Rappa had treated himself to now that he was retired: now that he didn't need them. He left the shop with the cuffs and the knife in its leather sheath, humming audibly.

At first he had augmented his young daughter's physiology with store-bought compounds, ones that he had labored over and experimented with when he wasn't at work and the children weren't at home, until they seemed as though they might produce the desired effect. Once the house in Queens had been purchased he had been able to grow the plants and process them with his own hands, in a superior fashion. The seeds and ovate leaves and the berries that grew in alongside them would enter the study and under Jimmy's watch would become something else entirely, a final product that was ground down and satisfyingly stripped of color. Now there was a locked curio cabinet in the study, and each of its five shelves was stocked with baskets upon baskets in which vials of the crystalline white powder waited as though they were little jars of spices. It is easy to hide such a thing in food.

Jimmy was saving the vials and was even producing more because he would need all of them in case of catastrophe, if they were forced to make their way on the road. When he pictured the end of the millennium he pictured Mari, who then would be almost eight. He should, he felt, be the one to guide her through the inevitable wasteland of the apocalypse. It would be them trudging along, burnt-out houses on either side, the houses' windows punched into sad black holes. Her mother he wouldn't bother with; she had rejected what he offered. "Do better," he'd commanded his son. "Find them," he'd said, not being so quick to believe the West Coast lie. Week after week and month after month he'd aimed lower until finally he had achieved results. "Luca Rappa," he had said on repeat. "You disgust me, figghiu miu. Show you're not a girl."

Of course before Y2K there would be the garden itself, too, for the girl to sit and lie in—contact with the plants having turned out to confer an amplifying effect. If his son was to be believed, Jimmy's granddaughter could come within inches of his daughter's face without becoming faint. The son had seen as much by trailing them in the street. Jimmy was sure that the child would require larger doses, longer exposures. He dedicated himself to making it possible.

*

One evening Jimmy took a taxi from Middle Village to the complex of arts-centered buildings on the Upper West Side. It was the opening night of the fiftieth anniversary season of the city's resident ballet company, and they were recreating their first performance. *Concerto Barocco* was on the docket, to be danced by a cast of eleven. So was *Orpheus* with its Dark Angel; so was *Symphony in C.* Jimmy sat in his handmade pinstripe trousers on a seat in one of the cheaper side boxes as he also had done when attending the premiere of *La Cenerentola.* The leading lady that night had been a servant in her own house, had been to Rossini the very image of bontà. On the opening night of the fiftieth anniversary the star to Jimmy was the dark celestial figure. He wondered when he would be able to bring his granddaughter to the opera, to the ballet.

In the daytime the old man busied himself with arranging the smallest of the bedrooms, which he emptied of the brown bags of groceries that he had piled there. He had burned Bice's things in a bonfire in the center of the garden years before; the ashes had discolored the ground. *September 24,* he had written in a cursive that resembled Shelley Script. *Today my daughter is dead, and her belongings with her.* He had looked in the mirror; he had blessed himself, without moving his lips or tongue. Now that he was expecting more consistent company than his son could offer, Jimmy became occupied with locating a rag rug to embellish the hard planks of the bedroom's wooden floor. He procured a white duvet cover sprigged with sage-green vines and a vanity mirror that swiveled and flipped with uninterrupted smoothness. He pictured the childish figure of the picciridda, who would grow taller and more substantial under his watch. Like the doors of the curio cabinet, the door to the room stayed closed and locked during his son's weekend visits.

With the slip of paper bearing the address of his daughter's current or former employer came the confidence Jimmy felt that he had no real need to rush. It was only natural that he should seek his one daughter: his beautiful daughter so like her mother who had died so soon after giving birth. The person who manned the front desk surely knew where his daughter lived and would surely tell him. Her place of residence, he believed in his bones, was still somewhere in New York. He took his time readying the room, the vials, the pawnshop treasures. He waited for the season of perpetual hope; it was a phrase he had heard in a movie aired on television. He waited until the low temperature reached 24 degrees. He pocketed the Smith & Wesson handcuffs and the semi-skinner knife.

*

At the American Youth Hostel, the proprietor and the young-adult travelers were also readying themselves for Christmas. Someone had bedecked the lobby of the hostel not just with artificial trees but with gaudy red and gold and green garlands and with plastic centerpieces pretending to be composed of holly and berries. At the front desk Jimmy remembered to ask after Brenda. The woman standing behind the check-in counter only hesitated for a moment before turning co-operative. "Brenda never mentioned," she said cheerfully, "that her father lived in town." Then she produced her own scrap of paper and on it scrawled the information the old man had so gently requested.

Apparently the closest cross street to the little girl's apartment was the street named for a Catholic saint whose identity no one could agree on: was he or was he not the man who had carried water to the house where god's one son had last eaten communally with friends? Nevertheless St. Mark had been deemed worthy of presiding over neighborhoods and churches and various international holidays and feasts. Having already been on the move with the handcuffs and the pearl-handled blade, Jimmy was only too happy to keep going to the spot he'd pinpointed on the map he carried with him: to make the trek from 103rd and Amsterdam.

*

The sound of the soles of Jimmy's shoes on the stairs echoed through the one cramped stairwell of the building, his feet thudding so heavily that a person could hear them even through the thick closed door of a small apartment. Inevitably it was the old man's granddaughter who answered the knock at the door: Mari, who had a month to go before turning seven and who continued to look eerily similar to her mother.

It had been four and a half years since the move, and Jimmy's daughter was starting to let her guard down again; she was not at home.

"Who are you?" the little girl asked.

The little girl may have been cautious but she wasn't shy, and the old man—who had brought with him a baked and iced dessert encased in plastic—gave her the look he gave all people he was meeting for the first time. The edges of his lips curled up symmetrically.

"Hello, niputi mia."

*

Despite all her warnings Jimmy's daughter had accidentally also trained his granddaughter to be kind, and that was why Mari had buzzed Jimmy in and opened the apartment door instead of pretending not to be at home. It was also how she ended up sitting at the drop-leaf table in the kitchen with the man who called her niputi, where he asked her for a cup of tea.

As he waited the old man's questions came swift and subtle. Did the little girl often stay home alone unaccompanied by her mother? Did they live there by themselves or with someone else? Was there—

here he paused almost imperceptibly—a man around that he should meet? Jimmy's granddaughter was tall enough both to reach the intercom and to make the tea while standing on a stool before the smallest gas stove that manufacturers had offered in the decade of her mother's birth. The apartment hadn't been renovated in the intervening time, and he noticed this as he surveyed the room and as the little girl filled the small, plain saucepan up with water. Of course the house on 67th Road had been and remained no better, but he found it vindicating that his daughter hadn't managed to improve her situation. 67th Road was what he talked of next.

"My mother won't be home for a long while," said the little girl, seemingly apropos of nothing.

The little girl climbed down from the stool and nudged it with her little foot, moving it far enough to the left that when she climbed up again she could open the door of the upper kitchen cabinet that held the teabags. "I was thinking," he said, "that when your mother returns we could take a trip to Middle Village."

She turned her head and gazed at him; she was all politeness.

"Or if you like," he said carefully, "we could make it an adventure, a surprise. Just this once," he said, "we could go without her."

The stove was not powerful, he inferred, and the water was taking its time in heating up.

"Come and have a bite of bundt cake," Jimmy suggested, removing the cake's plastic cover. Technically the sentence was a command. Technically the poison in the cake would only start a long and gradual process.

"Mancia, mancia, figghia mia," he said. "Why don't you bring us some plates?"

Rather than obeying the little girl stayed at the counter, placing teacups onto saucers and pouring sugar cubes into a dish, all the while asking questions like "When did you come to America?" and "How old are you, nannu?"—here was a word he'd taught her—and "What did my mother like to eat when she was small?"

It was the little girl's last question that made Jimmy pause and his smile fade. He looked away; he was remembering something unpleasant. Something that stayed with him long enough for his granddaughter to cross from the counter to the drop-leaf table and dump the boiling water for the tea into his lap.

Jimmy jumped up yelping and swatting at the little girl and she tried to dodge him and his hands. He was between her and the apartment door. She lunged and doubled back like a basketball player, hoping to fake him out. She was too slow. He had just caught and grabbed her when a key scraped at the lock.

The decoy mother that the little girl had described to Jimmy Rappa would leave her alone for hours at a time and had a mostly absent roomate. Neither of them had given him any reason to hurry. Jimmy's real daughter had only gone out for the things they would need the next morning: for milk and cheese and bread. This real Bice carried a folding knife of her own, a weapon her criminal friend must have given her, and without hesitation she reached for her purse. In an instant the knife was up against the neck of her father, who had spun around toward the door when she opened it, still clutching his granddaughter, and who now froze like a child with a snack he had been told not to take.

"Let—her—go," she said.

Jimmy put his hands up; she leaned in closer.

"Come back here again," she told him, "and I'll actually kill you."

Their faces were almost touching.

"If you go to the police," she told him, "I'll have you arrested."

He tried to raise an eyebrow, to look meaningfully at her.

"You know I could," Jimmy's daughter said.

She paused.

"And you know I will."

FAMOUS FAMIGLIA

Mari Rappa

The day my mother went after my grandfather with the knife was the day I knew that she had changed. At six years old I was serious, observant, and I had made up my mind that my grandfather was a criminal who was planning to abduct me when the only thing he had mentioned was how much I would like the row house where my mother had grown up. "The garden," he had said, "the garden is beautiful," and his eyes had gleamed and I had realized that he was looking at me and seeing not a child but a potted plant that he could cultivate. Understanding this I made casual conversation with my back turned; the aim was to keep him talking until my mother came home. If he believed it was an option he would want to befriend me. Too many people lived in our building for him to be able to carry me kicking and hollering out the door. In a way I believed that I had the situation under control. At the same time I could see how dangerous my grandfather was, how strategic. I would defy anyone to blame my mother for not escaping my grandfather as a child, for simply surviving under his spell.

After he was gone it was like a terrible malignance that had been inside my mother had been killed off and could no longer harm her. She didn't care when my uncle buzzed up having learned where we'd moved, or when he told us that my grandfather, in addition to nursing his burns, had taken ill with some mysterious disease. "He vomits bile," my uncle almost shouted at my mother over the intercom. "He stinks. What did you do?"

"No," she told him although it wasn't a polar question. No, she hadn't done a thing.

*

Y2K came and went and the world didn't end, and everyone was too relieved to talk about the truly apocalyptic threats. On January 3rd it was 64 degrees and my mother took me to the shrine by Grand Concourse and Villa Avenue because we'd missed the anniversary of the descent of Our Lady of Confidence. I'd never been in a church or read a bible but I knew the various names of the Mother Thrice Admirable, which I selected and used as I liked, turning them over in my head like polished gemstones from a box. On the way home we stopped off at Famiglia's and I chose two of the thickest rectangular slices that were named for the place we were from although their actual origins were more local. My mother has sometimes seemed uncomfortable claiming our island as hers, but I felt and feel connected to my grandmother who died and to her birthplace, and I was and am unwilling to give them up.

I turned nine, and my mother began the long process of telling me what had happened when her brother was my age and what had happened when she was. She cried while speaking; I didn't cry while listening. Then she told me the things my uncle had confessed to Gina one night at the diner, about his role in the sudden appearance of my grandfather at our apartment door. I asked her the essential question:

why did she want me to know this? She wanted me to know because I had to be prepared. She wanted me to know because on my tenth birthday a card would come in the mail and although she couldn't have predicted this event she sensed that there would be some development that would put me back in harm's way.

The card would be from my uncle; his father was dying and he was lonely. My uncle had listed an address below his name, which he had penciled in alongside the word *love*. The card described the warehouse as the perfect haven for a rebellious preteen. *If you ever need a place to go—*. The mailman had come while my mother was at work, and I tucked the card away before she could see it. It lay in a shoebox under my bed, my own bed because our roommate had moved out and finally we could afford all $830 of the stabilized rent. I was old enough to tell when my mother was tired from overwork although she always tried to deny it. "Mamma," I told her, "you don't have to lie. I'm not five; you can go to sleep." I told her she didn't always have to be some pillar of resolve. I think she started listening; some nights she fell asleep on the couch and I put myself to bed after her, feeling multiply accomplished.

Once I fought with my mother and the fight was particularly bad, and as she slammed my bedroom door I decided to unearth the card from under the little heaps of porcelain knickknacks and dried flowers and the ribbons I had piled on top of them in the box. I had visualized myself grabbing the card and flying out of the bedroom and then the apartment. Nothing was stopping me from taking the subway to the PATH train and the PATH train to the city across the water from Manhattan. Instead I sat on the bed with the card for half an hour, thinking, before placing it again into the box and pushing the box back under the bed, further away this time. That afternoon and in the afternoons that followed I started pursuing a writing project of my own.

At first the sketches were short: they were flashes of my mother arriving in Middle Village and the butcher not knowing whether to love or fear her and my grandfather forcing her to eat. When I was finished for the night I would feel a little ashamed, as though I'd done something wrong by connecting dots I couldn't fully comprehend, as well as more than a little euphoric, as though I'd beaten up a school-yard bully or vanquished a curse. I felt the strange horror and the strange familiarity of these lives that were also mine.

When I did go to Hoboken it was to interview Gina, whom I thought of as an aunt and who had long since moved out of the warehouse. I walked by myself around Middle Village, where I wasn't afraid to go because I could take care of myself. In this way I saw the places that had shaped my mother and I saw them on my own terms. Things there often were distantly beautiful or charming and then turned ugly up close. I went home and crumpled up whole pages of handwritten lines, tossing them into the wastebasket under the second-hand desk that once had belonged to our roommate. I wrote the pages over again; I tried to make them true. My fictional mother was angry, then panicked. My uncle alternately hated and excused and hated himself; he couldn't make up his mind. Anxiety and compulsion were an itch that made him break out in cold sweats when he didn't scratch it. I was the girl whose mother had finally escaped. *C'era una volta*, I wrote. I was teaching myself to talk like my mother's bambinaia.

*

Today there are things that have altered and things that haven't. This is not a story of my grandfather's redemption; still dying, he continues not to deserve to be redeemed. After one too many harangues my uncle showed up again at our place off St. Marks. "I'd rather be here with you," he told us, looking down at the brown bristles of our welcome mat. "Please let me," he said, not trying to barge in. I glanced at my mother and my mother glanced at me and we moved to either side of the doorway so that he could step into the kitchen. Now at dinner we stuff our faces with pani and ragù as he worries audibly, narrating his thoughts and dreams in vivid and rueful and comic detail. "You don't need fixing," we tell him in near-unison, *we* being my mother and I and often Gina. My surrogate aunt teases my mother about the butcher, about not having been able to stay away. It will be impossible for my grandfather to rise up again and hurt us when we aren't looking, because we're always looking; we're never not ready.

I want my mother to allow herself the things she never has. I tell her there are people who might surprise her, that kissing isn't everything—here she blushes—and that even if it was, there might be someone in this mad world who's like me: immune to the person her father made her. I watch her at the grocery store or on the subway when it's crowded and I see people cross into the bubble that my mother claims she needs to keep from making strangers convulse and retch. I scrutinize their movements and, not seeing them get sick, I start to wonder if my mother's condition hasn't improved in the years since she breathed in my grandfather's face. Maybe it takes the help of a daughter's daughter to reverse what a patriarch has done. The idea pleases me although if there's a truth to know about this part of my mother then I'm afraid I may never find out. She's not the person she was when she was twenty-six and wanted to fool herself into believing that she could be reckless like her only friend. Multiple times she's refused to test my theory, to risk making another person throw up.

I've told my mother what she should give me when I turn eighteen and leave for the gray stone campus that starts at 130th Street and ends at 141ˢᵗ. For two years I've been marking up their course catalog with highlighters in neon shades of orange and blue and green, and maybe I've read too many of my mother's translated papers, but I think the kinds of novels I want to learn to write are the ones that envision solutions for a ravaged planet. On the other hand I'm afraid of being all ideas, of never following through. This is what I'm thinking about when I buy the bouquet of flowers from the supermarket and bring them home to my mother, who is sitting on the couch.

"You promised," I remind her; it's the date I was born. She starts to protest, then stops before words can escape. I think she loves me enough to believe that I might be right.

Instead of speaking she takes one flower, a tulip. The stem is in her hand; the bloom is yellow and red. I watch her bring the clump of petals within range.

She opens her mouth and exhales.

ACKNOWLEDGMENTS

I am grateful to the editors of *Cherry Tree*, *failbetter*, *Gone Lawn*, *J Journal*, *Necessary Fiction*, *South Carolina Review*, and *Sundog Lit*, where excerpts from this book originally appeared. In "First Night at Fern's Spectacular Twenty-Four-Hour Diner," the italicized phrases "at sixteen, he ran away from home" and "signs of economic distress and decay" are quoted with permission from Eric Foner's *Tom Paine and Revolutionary America* (OUP 2005). Special thanks go to my husband Jonny for his incredibly perceptive readings and re-readings of every chapter of this novel from "Mulberry" to "Famous Famiglia," and for his exquisite typesetting, book design, and cover design; to my almost-twin and brilliant fellow writer Ann Hoag for her endless encouragement and infectious laugh; to the formidable Dana Murphy for her solidarity and for sharing her artistic and scholarly genius with me; to Sander and Remy for lighting up every moment when I'm not writing and many of the ones when I am; and to the multiple generations of women on both sides of my family whose stories in various guises are represented in these pages.

SUZANNE MANIZZA ROSZAK is a writer and teacher living in Groningen, the Netherlands. Raised in rural Connecticut, she spent eight years in New York City with stints in Palo Alto and Hoboken before moving to Long Beach, California. While in school, she worked a series of jobs as a caterer's helper, a waitress, a short-order cook, an office assistant, a barista, a tutor, and a copyeditor. Suzanne holds an MFA in creative writing from the University of California, Irvine and a PhD in comparative literature from Yale. Her fiction, creative nonfiction, and poetry have appeared in *ANMLY*, *Bellingham Review*, *Colorado Review*, *DIAGRAM*, *failbetter*, *Jabberwock Review*, *New Letters*, *Third Coast*, and elsewhere. Her poetry collection *Sicilianas* won the 2022 Lauria/Frasca Poetry Prize from Bordighera Press and was first finalist for the North American Poetry Book Award.